EARTH FACTS

Lynn Bresler

CONTENTS

Designed by Teresa Foster

**Illustrated by Tony Gibson
and Ian Jackson**

With thanks to Chris Rice and Stephen Capus

Earth's vital statistics

Earth's place in the Universe

Our galaxy is one of 400 million galaxies in the Universe. The small part of our galaxy which you can see in the sky is called the Milky Way. It contains over 3,000 million stars. If each star was a full stop, like this, . . . they would make a line stretching from London to Moscow.

Earth statistics

Diameter:	
at the Poles	12,713 km
at the Equator	12,756 km
Circumference:	
round the Poles	40,000 km
round the Equator	40,075 km
Density:	5.518g/cm^3
Volume:	1.08 x 10^{12} km^3
Total surface area: 510,066,000 sq km	
Weight: 6,000 million million million tonnes	

The solar system

The Sun is one of the stars in the Milky Way. Nine planets revolve around it. Scientists think the Sun and planets were all formed about 4,600 million years ago.

The Earth's Moon

The Earth is the third nearest planet to the Sun. It has one natural satellite orbiting it, the Moon, which is 384,365 km (238,840 miles) from the Earth. The Moon is a quarter the size of the Earth.

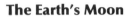

The short way round

The Earth is not a true sphere. It is slightly flattened at the top and bottom. The diameter through the Poles is 43 km (26 miles) less than it is at the Equator.

Watery Earth

About 70 per cent of the Earth's surface is covered in water. The southern hemisphere is more watery than the northern hemisphere. Over 80 per cent of the people on Earth live north of the Equator.

The Continents

Continent	Area in sq km
Asia	44,391,200
Africa	30,244,000
North America	24,247,000
South America	17,821,000
Antarctica	13,338,500
Europe	10,354,600
Oceania	8,547,000

Faraway

The 299 people on Tristan da Cunha, in the Atlantic Ocean, live on the most isolated inhabited island on Earth. Their nearest neighbours are on the island of St Helena, 2,120 km (1,320 miles) away.

Bouvey Oya, in the South Atlantic Ocean, is the most isolated uninhabited island on Earth. It is 1,700 km (1,050 miles) from the east coast of Antarctica.

New land

New islands are still being formed by volcanoes erupting under the sea. Surtsey emerged from the sea off the coast of Iceland in 1963. The newest island is Lateiki, off the east coast of Australia, which was first spotted in 1979.

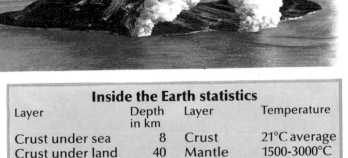

Surtsey

Largest islands

Island	Area in sq km
Greenland	2,175,000
New Guinea	789,900
Borneo	751,000
Madagascar	587,000
Baffin	507,400
Sumatra	422,200
Honshu	230,000
Great Britain	229,800
Victoria	217,300
Ellesmere	196,200

DID YOU KNOW?

The Pacific Ocean, the largest ocean, is three times bigger than Asia, the largest continent.

Inside the Earth

The surface of the Earth is a thin crust of rock. Under this, scientists believe, is a layer of liquid rock, the mantle, which surrounds an outer core of liquid iron and nickel. The inner core at the centre of the Earth is probably a solid ball of iron and nickel.

Inside the Earth statistics

Layer	Depth in km	Layer	Temperature
Crust under sea	8	Crust	21°C average
Crust under land	40	Mantle	1500-3000°C
Mantle	2,870	Outer core	3900°C
Outer core	2,100	Inner core	4000°C
Inner core	1,370 (radius)		

The Earth's history

In the beginning

Scientists think that the Earth was formed, about 4,600 million years ago, from a spinning cloud of dust and gases, which shrank to a hot, molten globe. As this cooled, a crust of rock formed on the surface. The oldest of the Earth's rocks are in west Greenland, and are 3,820 million years old.

Jigsaw

The crust of the Earth is not one solid piece. It is cracked into a jigsaw of 7 huge pieces, and several smaller ones. The pieces, called plates, are about 64 km (40 miles) thick. The plates float on the hot, liquid rock of the mantle, the deep layer beneath the crust.

Bump! Crunch!

The cracked, jigsaw pieces of the crust have drifted on the surface of the Earth for millions of years. Where the plates bumped and collided, the crust crumpled – forming deep trenches in the sea floor, and forcing the rocks up to form mountains on the land. Some of the land is still rising – Tibet has risen over 3 km (2 miles) in the last 2 million years.

Slip sliding away

The plates can slip past each other on land, as well as under the sea. The San Andreas Fault, in the USA, a boundary between 2 plates, is a great crack, stretching for 1,126 km (700 miles) from the Gulf of California. Over 15 million years, California has moved about 300 km (186 miles) north-westwards, and in 50 million years' time, might have split away.

The changing crust

New crust is being made all the time on the sea floor. Hot, liquid rock bubbles up through the huge cracks between the plates, such as the ridge in the middle of the Atlantic Ocean. As much as 10 cm (4 in) of new rock a year can be formed, on either side of the crack.

The ridge is close to the surface underneath Iceland. The island is expanding very slowly, where liquid rock spills out from great cracks which run across the island.

In other places on the sea floor, the plates slide over each other. This forces some of the crust down deep sea trenches, such as the Peru-Chile Trench in the Pacific Ocean, back into the hot mantle.

Continental drift

The drifting of the Earth's crust means the continents have not always been in the same place. North Africa was once covered in a sheet of ice and was where the South Pole is today. And the South Pole was once covered with rain forests.

Yesterday

About 200 million years ago, most of the land was probably joined up into a large continent, called Pangaea. This split into two – Laurasia, now mainly in the northern hemisphere, and Gondwanaland, now mainly in the southern.

Today

The continents are still moving today. In 50 million years' time, Alaska and the USSR may have joined together.

Tomorrow?

Wearing away

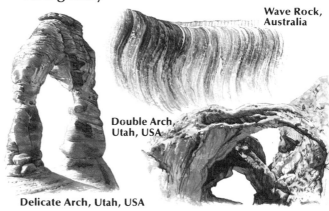

Wave Rock, Australia

Double Arch, Utah, USA

Delicate Arch, Utah, USA

The landscape has changed over millions of years. Erosion by ice, wind and water has worn away the surface of the Earth. Glaciers have carved valleys, fjords and jagged mountain peaks. Rivers have carved great canyons, such as the Grand Canyon in Colorado, USA, which is 349 km (217 miles) long. Rain and wind have sculpted cliffs, such as Wave Rock in Australia, and natural arches, such as Delicate Arch, in Utah, USA.

All change!

The people on Earth have changed the landscape too. They have cleared forests, straightened rivers, and terraced steep hillsides for farming. They have quarried rocks, metals and minerals out of the ground. The Bingham Canyon copper mine in Utah, USA, has created a hole 3.7 km (2.3 miles) across and 789 m (2,590 ft) deep. People have also created new land, by reclaiming land from the sea, such as one-third of the farm land in The Netherlands.

The Earth's atmosphere

Outside the Earth

The Earth is surrounded by a blanket of air, called the atmosphere, which is divided into different layers. The highest reaches up into Space, 8,000 km (5,000 miles) above the Earth.

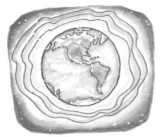

In the beginning

The Earth's atmosphere was originally a hot, steamy mixture of gases. Scientists think that it was made up of gases such as methane, nitrogen, hydrogen and carbon dioxide, as well as water vapour.

DID YOU KNOW?

There is enough water in the atmosphere, that if it all fell as rain at the same time, it would cover the entire surface of the Earth with 2.5 cm (1 in) of water.

Oxygen – the air that we breathe

Oxygen was first formed only about 2,000 million years ago, when plants, called algae, started to appear on the Earth. Plants produce oxygen in sunlight, which animals, including people, breathe in. All animals breathe out carbon dioxide, which plants breathe in.

Gasping for air

The higher you go, the thinner the air, which is why mountaineers need extra oxygen. The density of air at the top of Everest is only about one-third that at sea level.

Atmospheric heights

Layer	Height above Earth
Exosphere	500-8,000 km
Thermosphere	80-500 km
Mesosphere	50-80 km
Stratosphere	8-50 km
Troposphere (over Equator)	16 km
(over Poles)	8 km

What is the atmosphere made of?

The highest layer, the exosphere, is probably made mostly of helium, hydrogen and oxygen.

The lower layers are made of:

Gas	Per cent
Nitrogen	75.51
Oxygen	23.15
Argon	1.28
Carbon dioxide	
Neon	
Helium	
Krypton	.06
Hydrogen	
Xenon	
Ozone	

Plus water vapour, and microscopic dust particles, plant spores and pollen grain

Atmospheric temperatures

Layer	Temperature
Exosphere	2200°C minimum
Thermosphere	−80°C to 2,200°C
Mesosphere	10°C to −80°C
Stratosphere	−55°C to 10°C
Troposphere	
(at 16 km high)	−55°C
(at sea level)	15°C

Dust high

A giant volcanic eruption can throw dust and ash as high as the stratosphere. The dust and ash can travel halfway around the world, and take as long as three years to fall back to Earth.

Bouncing waves

Radio signals move at the speed of light, 300,000 km (186,420 miles) per second. The signals can travel around the curve of the Earth, by bouncing off the electrically-charged air in the mesosphere and thermosphere.

Flying high

The troposphere is the storm, wind and cloud layer. Planes fly high above the weather, in the stratosphere, where they use air currents, called jet streams, which can blow at up to 483 km (300 miles) per hour. Most of the jet streams blow from west to east.

Force of gravity

The atmosphere is held to the Earth by the force of gravity. Astronauts have to travel through the atmosphere at more than 27,360 km (17,000 miles) per hour to break free of Earth's gravity.

Record heights

	Height above Earth
Unmanned balloon	52 km
Mig-25 fighter plane	38 km
Manned balloon	35 km
Concorde	18 km
747 Jumbo jet	12 km
DC9 plane	8 km

In comparison, Mount Everest is 9 km high.

Sunscreen

Up in the stratosphere, 24 km (15 miles) above the Earth, is the ozone layer. This filters out the Sun's harmful ultra-violet rays – without the ozone, life would not survive on Earth.

Mountains

High ground

About 25 per cent of the Earth's land surface is 914 m (3,000 ft) or more above sea level. Of this, most of the continent of Antarctica is about 1,829 m (6,000 ft) high and the country of Tibet averages 4,572 m (15,000 ft) high.

Capital fact

The highest capital city in the world is La Paz, in Bolivia. It is 3,625 m (11,893 ft) up in the Andes.

Avalanche!

The slam of a car door, a falling branch or the movement of a skier can start an avalanche. The snow can slide down at a speed of 322 km (200 miles) an hour.

High living

There is less oxygen the higher up you go. Mountain people and animals can live at great heights because they have bigger hearts and lungs, which carry more blood, and therefore more oxygen.

Quechua Indians live 3,650 m (12,000 ft) up in the Andes, where they grow potatoes and corn, and herd sheep.

Mountain heights

People and wildlife can survive at different heights up a mountain. This shows some of the life of the Himalayas.

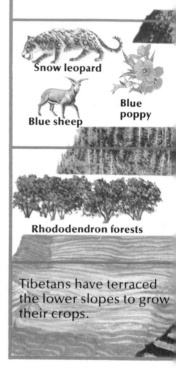

Snow leopard

Blue sheep

Blue poppy

Rhododendron forests

Tibetans have terraced the lower slopes to grow their crops.

Cliff climbers

Rocky Mountain goats can climb up cliffs which are almost vertical. Tough pads on their hooves act as suction cups, and stop them from slipping on the steep rocks.

Highest mountain by continent

Continent	Location	Mountain	Height
Asia	Nepal/Tibet	Everest	8,848 m
Africa	Tanzania	Kilimanjaro	5,895 m
North America	Alaska	McKinley	6,194 m
South America	Argentina	Aconcagua	6,960 m
Antarctica	Ellsworth Land	Vinson Massif	5,140 m
Western Europe	France	Mont Blanc	4,810 m
Eastern Europe	USSR	Elbrus	5,633 m
Oceania	New Zealand	Cook	3,764 m

7,600 m (25,000 ft)

Springtail   Alpine chough

Jumping spider Cushion pinks

4,900 m (16,000 ft)

Tibetans take their yaks up as high as 4,600 m (15,000 ft) to graze during the summer.

3,000 m (10,000 ft)

Red panda   Asian black bear

1,200 m (4,000 ft)

Longest mountain ranges

Range	Location	Length
Andes	South America	7,240 km
Rockies	North America	6,030 km
Himalaya/Karakoram/ HinduKush	Asia	3,860 km
Great Dividing Range	Australia	3,620 km
Trans-Antarctic	Antarctica	3,540 km

The Andes are over twice as long as North America is wide.

Mountain climate

The higher you go up a mountain, the colder it gets. The temperature drops by 2°C (3.6°F) for every 300 m (984 ft) of height. The temperature is as low as −20°C (−4°F) at the top of the Himalayas, where fierce winds can reach over 300 km (186 miles) an hour.

DID YOU KNOW?

Seashells can be found in rocks high up on some mountains, such as the Apennines in Italy. The rocks were once at the bottom of the sea. They were pushed upwards over millions of years, as the crust of the Earth crumpled.

Changing shape

As they get older, mountains gradually change shape. Frost and ice split and wear away the rock. Scientists think mountains lose about 8.6 cm (3½ in) every 1,000 years.

Mountain ages

Mountain ranges are millions of years old, but they are not all the same age.

Scientists have worked out the approximate age of mountain ranges. Here are some examples.

Million years old	Location	Mountain range
400	Scotland	Highlands
250	USA	Appalachians
	USSR	Urals
80	South America	Andes
70	North America	Rockies
40	Asia	Himalayas
15	Europe	Alps

Tundra

Frozen prairie

The frozen prairie, the flat tundra, stretches between the tree line (the northern edge of forest lands) and the Arctic polar region. It is almost 1½ times the size of Brazil, covering nearly one-tenth of the Earth's land surface, including northern Canada, Norway, Sweden, Finland and Greenland, Siberia, Alaska and Iceland.

Soggy landscape

The tundra has only about 20 cm (8 in) of rain a year. The permafrost stops the water from draining away, so about half the area of tundra is dotted with marshes and shallow lakes. Only the top few cms of tundra thaw each summer.

Northern dawn

The ghostly lights of the Aurora borealis shimmer and glow high in the atmosphere in the far north. Curtains and streamers of light move across the winter skies.

Tundra people

About 90,000 Eskimos live in the tundra area. Most of them now live in wooden houses, but in Greenland and Canada, a few still live in igloos. Other tundra dwellers include 300,000 Yakuts in Siberia and 30,000 Lapps in Scandinavia.

Commuter caribou

Herds of caribou, as many as 100,000 in each herd, trek 600 km (373 miles) north to the tundra every spring, where the young caribou are born. As summer ends, they return south, following routes they have used for centuries.

Amazing But True

Scientists were able to make a 10,000-year-old seed germinate and sprout. The Arctic lupin seed was found in Yukon, in Canada.

Tundra statistics	
Area of tundra	13,000,000 sq km
Depth of permafrost	305-610 m
Temperature	
Winter	−29 to −34°C
Summer	3 to 12°C

Winter white

Many of the birds and animals which live on the tundra all year round change colour according to the season. In autumn they turn white to match the snow; in spring, they change back to their summer colours.

Arctic fox

Snowy owl

Snowshoe rabbit

Stoat

Arctic hare

Ptarmigan

The Trans-Alaskan oil pipeline stretches 1,300 km (800 miles) from the Arctic Ocean to southern Alaska. The oil is heated to at least 45°C (130°F), to stop it freezing in the pipe.

Buzz off!

In calm weather, during the short summer, plagues of mosquitoes and other flies infest the tundra. Warble flies are so ferocious, they can cause madness in some of the caribou herds.

Deep freeze

The permafrost can act as a deep freeze. Ice Age mammoths have been found in Siberia. And the body of John Torrington, a British naval officer who died in 1845, on an expedition to the Bering Strait, was found in 1983.

Colder than ice

In the winter, under its blanket of ice and snow, the tundra in north-east Siberia is colder, at −70°C (−94°F), than it is at the North Pole.

Permafrost

The permafrost, the deep layer of ground beneath the tundra, is frozen all the year round. A layer as much as 1,500 m (4,921 ft) deep has been recorded in Siberia.

Low life

You can walk on top of the tundra forests. Near to the tree line, the trees are so blasted by the cold, dry winds, they grow close to the ground. Branches of ground willow can be up to 5 m (16 ft) in length, but they only rise above the surface by about 10 cm (4 in).

Forests . . . 1

Coniferous trees

Coniferous trees have cones and needle-like leaves. Most conifers are evergreen, but some, such as larches, lose their needles in the autumn. Coniferous forests grow in colder climates in the far north, and high up on mountains – even those in the Tropics.

Broad-leaved trees

Broad-leaved trees have flowers and wide, flat leaves. Some broad-leaved trees are deciduous, they lose their leaves in autumn; others are evergreen. Deciduous broad-leaved forests grow in warm, temperate climates. Evergreen broad-leaved forests grow where it is hot and wet all the time.

Forest statistics

Coniferous forests stretch across northern Europe, Asia and North America, and are found in mountain regions, such as the Rockies, Alps and Urals. Mixed and deciduous broad-leaved forests are found mostly in west and central Europe, eastern USA, and parts of Japan, China and New Zealand.

Type of forest	Type of trees
Coniferous	Conifers
Mixed	Deciduous broad-leaved/conifers
Deciduous	Deciduous broad-leaved
Tropical rain	Evergreen broad-leaved

The tropical rain forests equal all the other forest types added together.

Timber merchant

Coniferous trees supply almost three-quarters of the world's timber, as well as nearly all the paper used. It takes one tree to produce 270 copies of a 190-page paperback book.

Rooted deep

Hickory trees grow to 37 m (120 ft) tall. The main root, the taproot, could be as long as 30 m (100 ft) – the root may be nearly as deep as the tree is high.

Coniferous forest trees

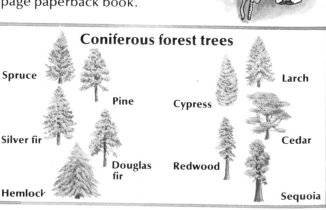

Spruce

Silver fir

Pine

Douglas fir

Hemlock

Cypress

Redwood

Larch

Cedar

Sequoia

Deciduous broad-leaved forest trees

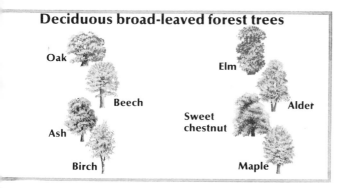

Oak
Elm
Beech
Alder
Ash
Sweet chestnut
Birch
Maple

Oldest, largest, tallest

The mountain forests of north-west America have the oldest and the largest and the tallest trees on Earth.

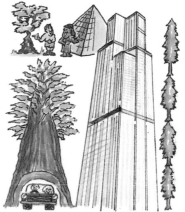

Fire-proof trees

Fires can burn forests at a rate of up to 15 km (10 miles) an hour, and the roar of the fire can be heard 1.6 km (1 mile) away. Trees protected by very thick bark, for example pine and sequoia, are only scarred by the fire, the wood is undamaged.

Woodlands

Woodland flowers bloom in the spring, before the trees come into leaf and block most of the sunlight. When the leaves fall in autumn they rot, forming humus, which makes the soil more fertile.

Crops from coniferous trees

Part of tree	Some examples of use
Timber	Furniture
	Matches
	Tannic acid
Pulp	Paper
	Plastics
	Rayon
Cellulose	Cellophane
	Turpentine
Needles	Pine-leaf oil (used in soap)
	Vitamins A and E

Amazing But True

Each year, every person in the USA uses up enough items made from wood to equal a tree 30 m (100 ft) tall and 41 cm (16 in) in diameter. That adds up to over 230 million trees a year.

Bristlecone pines nearly 5,000 years old, about the same age as the Pyramids in Egypt. Giant sequoias up to 7.6 m (26 ft) across - wide enough to drive a car through. Redwoods up to 107 m (350 ft) tall. Four balanced on top of each other would be nearly as high as the Sears Roebuck Tower, the world's tallest building.

Giant cone

The largest pine cones grow on the sugar pine trees of the USA. They reach 66 cm (26 in) long, nearly two-thirds the length of a baseball bat.

13

Forests . . . 2

Tropical rain forests

Rain forests cover about 6 per cent of the Earth's land surface. A hundred million years ago, rain forests grew in Norway. Today, they are mostly on or south of the Equator, for example in New Guinea, Malaysia and parts of Africa, Burma, Indonesia and South America.

Treeless forests

Great forests of bamboo, over 18 m (60 ft) high, grow in the south-western mountains of China, where giant pandas live. Bamboo is not a tree, it is a type of grass. Field grass grows to an average of only 100 cm (39 in).

Flying frogs

Asian tree frogs (10 cm, 4 in long) can "fly" from one tree to another, as much as 12 m (40 ft) away. The webs of skin between their toes act as parachutes.

DID YOU KNOW?

About 2,500 million people, half the world's population, use wood for cooking and heating.

Daily rain

It rains nearly every day in the tropical rain forests. At least 203 cm (80 in) and as much as 381 cm (150 in) can fall each year. The temperature rarely drops below 26.6°C (80°F) and the air is 80 per cent moisture.

Slowcoach

In the forests of South America is the slowest moving land mammal. The sloth spends much of its time hanging upside-down from trees When it does move, it creeps along at 2 m (7 ft) a minute.

Rain forest layers

The plants and trees in the tropical rain forests grow up to different heights. The forest can be divided into five "layers".

Layer	Height
Attic	up to 91 m
Canopy	46-76 m
Understorey	6-12 m
Shrub	0.6-6 m
Herb	up to 0.6 m

Bush ropes

Bush ropes, or lianas, hang down from the rain forest canopy. They can be 60 cm (2 ft) thick and as much as 152 m (500 ft) long, and are strong enough to swing on.

Perching plants

Perching plants grow on trees high up in the canopy, where they absorb food and moisture from the air. Plants, such as bromeliads, can provide a home for insects and frogs, 70 m (230 ft) above the forest floor.

Life in the rain forest

Only 1 per cent of sunlight reaches the rain forest floor. So most of the insects, birds and animals have to live up in the canopy, where there is more sunlight and food.

Amazing But True

Tree kangaroos live in the New Guinea forests. They mostly live up in the trees, but can jump down to the forest floor from a height of 18 m (59 ft). Their tails are longer than their bodies.

Rain forest crops

The Earth's rain forests supply many of our crops. Rubber, lacquer, gum, waxes and dyes can all be made from rain forest trees. Here are some other examples.

Timber	Mahogany
	Teak
Fruit	Bananas
	Pineapples
Spices	Paprika
	Pepper
Oils	Palm
	Patchouli
Fibres	Jute
	Rattan
Beans	Coffee
	Cocoa

Cloud forest giants

Giant plants grow 3,000 m (9,842 ft) up in the cloud forests on Mount Kenya, where the trees are blanketed in fog and mist. Groundsel, over 6 m (20 ft) high, look like giant cabbages on trunks. Lobelias, up to 8 m (26 ft) tall, look like furry columns because of their hairy leaves.

Medicine cabinet

Some of our medicines are made from rain forest trees. Quinine and aspirin are made from tree bark; cough mixture is made from tree resin.

Lakes and rivers

Drop of water

Only 3 per cent of all the water on Earth is fresh; the rest is salty. Of that 3 per cent, over 2 per cent is frozen in ice sheets and glaciers; so less than 1 per cent is in lakes, rivers and under the ground.

Longest rivers by continent

Continent	Country	River	Lengtn
Asia	China	Yangtze	5,520 km
Africa	Egypt	Nile	6,670 km
North America	USA	Mississippi/ Missouri	6,020 km
South America	Brazil	Amazon	6,437 km
Eastern Europe	USSR	Volga	3,688 km
Western Europe	Germany	Rhine	1,320 km
Oceania	Australia	Murray/Darling	3,720 km

Some of the rivers flow through more than one country. Most of each river is in the country listed.

DID YOU KNOW?

Not all rivers end up in an ocean. The rivers flowing south from the Tassili Mountains in north Africa, slow down to a trickle and disappear into the dry Sahara sands.

Deepest lake

Lake Baikal, in the USSR, is 644 km (400 miles) long and 48 km (30 miles) wide. It is so deep, ranging from 1,620-1,940 m (5,315-6,365 ft), that all five of the Great Lakes in North America could be emptied into it.

Amazing But True

Piranhas are ferocious, flesh-eating fish. Their triangular teeth are so sharp, the Amazonian Indians use them as scissors.

Living afloat

One of the highest lakes is Titicaca, 3,810 m (12,500 ft) up in the Peruvian Andes. There are "floating" islands on the lake, some as big as football fields, made from thickly matted totora reeds. People live on the islands, and build their houses, boats and baskets from the reeds – and they eat the roots of the reeds too.

Highest waterfalls

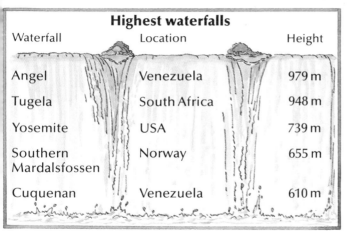

Waterfall	Location	Height
Angel	Venezuela	979 m
Tugela	South Africa	948 m
Yosemite	USA	739 m
Southern Mardalsfossen	Norway	655 m
Cuquenan	Venezuela	610 m

The mighty Amazon

The Amazon is the greatest river on Earth. It starts 5,200 m (17,000 ft) up in the snows of the Andes, and ends 6,437 km (4,000 miles) later on the Atlantic coast, in a maze of islands and channels, 300 km (186 miles) wide.

The Amazon's flow of water is so great, one-fifth of all river water, that the freshwater stretches 180 km (112 miles) out to sea, colouring the sea with yellow-brown silt.

Niagara on the move

Niagara Falls are midway along the Niagara River, which flows between Lakes Ontario and Erie. The Falls date back 10,000 years, to the end of the last Ice Age.

At that time they were 11 km (7 miles) further downriver; the pounding water has gradually worn away the rocks at the edge of the Falls. In about 25,000 years' time, Niagara will disappear when the Falls reach Lake Erie – and the Lake may drain away.

Busy waterfall

The Iguazu Falls in Brazil are 4 km (2½ miles) wide and 80 m (260 ft) high. During the rainy season, November to March, the amount of water pouring over the Falls every second would fill about 6 Olympic-size swimming pools.

Largest lakes and inland seas

Most lakes contain freshwater, but two of the largest – the Aral and the Caspian – are really inland seas, as they contain saltwater.

Lake/inland sea	Location	Size
Caspian Sea	Iran/USSR	372,000 sq km
Superior	Canada/USA	82,414 sq km
Victoria	East Africa	69,485 sq km
Aral Sea	USSR	66,500 sq km
Huron	Canada/USA	59,596 sq km
Michigan	USA	58,016 sq km
Tanganyika	East Africa	32,893 sq km

Grasslands and savannahs

Grassy places

Grasslands and savannahs cover about one-quarter of the land on Earth. Savannahs have patches of grass, up to 4.5 m (15 ft) tall, and scrub, bushes and a few small trees. Grasslands can be used for growing crops, such as wheat, or as pasture, for grazing animals. The grass height ranges from 30-215 cm (1-7 ft).

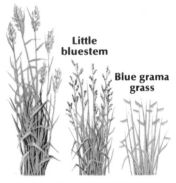

Indian grass

Little bluestem

Blue grama grass

Grassy names

Grasslands and savannahs are called different names in different parts of the world. These are some examples.

Grasslands

Country	Name
Argentina	Pampas
North America	Prairie
South Africa	Veldt
Central Asia	Steppes
Australia	Scrub

Savannahs

Country	Name
East Africa	Savannah
Brazil	Campo
Venezuela	Llanos

DID YOU KNOW?

The largest wheatfield, in Alberta, Canada, covered an area of 142 sq km (55 sq miles). That added up to nearly 20,000 soccer pitches.

Grasslands

There are grasslands in Europe, Asia, North America, South America, South Africa and Australia in areas where there is too little rain for forests to grow, but enough rain to stop the land turning to desert.

Grasslands have hot summers and cold winters. In the North American prairies, the temperature in winter can drop to freezing (0°C, 32°F) and climb to 38°C (100°F) in summer. Rainfall can vary between 50-100 cm (20-40 in) a year.

All about grasses

There are about 10,000 different kinds of grass on Earth. Most grasses have hollow stems, although some have solid stems, such as maize and sugar cane.

Grasses are flowering plants, but are pollinated by the wind carrying pollen from flower to flower. So grasses do not need brightly coloured flowers to attract insects to carry the pollen.

New grass

Grass fires, which can be sparked off by lightning, can destroy grass stems, but the grass soon grows back again. The growing point of grass is so close to the ground, at the base of the leaves, that it does not get burnt – or even eaten by animals as they graze the grass.

Crops

Cereal crops have been developed by people from wild grasses. They are used as food for people and for animals. Here are some examples.

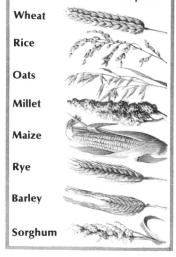

Wheat

Rice

Oats

Millet

Maize

Rye

Barley

Sorghum

Savannah choice

Different animals on the savannah eat different plants. Giraffes feed on branches high in trees; antelopes feed on lower branches. Zebras eat the tops of grasses; wildebeest eat the rest of the stem; and gazelles eat the young shoots.

Rice

Rice is the only grass which can grow in water, and is the main food of more than half the world's population. Almost all of the rice – about 90 per cent – is grown in Asia.

Upside-down trees

The baobab trees of Africa have enormous, swollen trunks, in which water is stored, topped by short, stumpy branches which look more like tree roots. Old trees are sometimes hollow, and have been used as bus shelters – or even as houses.

Savannahs

Savannahs are mostly near the Equator, in Africa, South-East Asia and India, and in Australia, in areas where it is warm all the year round. Some savannahs are dry for as much as 10 months of the year, with only 20 cm (8 in) of rain. Others are dry for only 3 months, with as much as 120 cm (47 in) of rain.

Staying alive

The colours of animals living in savannahs help to protect them from predators, but also hides the predators themselves. Striped or spotted animals, such as cheetahs and leopards, are difficult to see from a distance, especially when they move through sunlight and shadow. The tawny colour of a lion hides it in the long, dry grass.

Deserts

What is a desert?

A desert is an area which has less than 25 cm (10 in) of rain a year, and very little plant life. In some deserts, the total rain for the year might fall in only two or three storms. But that is enough for plant seeds to sprout and bloom, turning parts of the desert into carpets of flowers for a few days.

Largest deserts		Size in sq km
Desert	Location	
Sahara	North Africa	8,400,000
Australian	Australia	1,550,000
Arabian	South-West Asia	1,300,000
Gobi	Central Asia	1,040,000
Patagonia	South America	670,000
Kalahari	Southern Africa	520,000
Turkestan	Central Asia	450,000
Takla Makan	China	320,000
Sonoran	USA/Mexico	310,000
Namib	South-West Africa	310,000

Deserted places

Deserts cover about 20 per cent of the Earth's land surface. Many desert areas are bare rock, or are covered with pebbles and gravel. Sand accounts for only about 15 per cent of the Earth's desert regions.

Colossal cacti

Cacti are found only in American deserts. The tallest are saguaros which can reach 15 m (50 ft) tall, weigh 7 tons and live for 200 years. Water is stored in the stem and used in times of drought.

The driest land

The Atacama in northern Chile is the driest desert on Earth. Parts of the desert had no rain for 400 years, from 1570-1971, and in other parts, rain has never been recorded.

Death Valley

WATER 100KM

At 57°C (134°F), Death Valley is the driest, hottest place in North America. Gold prospectors died there, in 1849, when they ran out of food and water on their way to the Californian goldfields – which is how the Valley got its name.

Sandstorm

One of the sandiest deserts is the Takla Makan. Sandstorms can whip up the sand as high as 3,048 m (10,000 ft). Wind-blown sand in the Sahara can be so fierce, it will sandblast the paint off a car or aeroplane.

Hot and cold deserts

There are 10 major desert regions. "Cold" deserts have hot summers and relatively cold winters. "Hot" deserts are hot during the day, all the year round.

Cold deserts
West/south-west North
   America
Patagonia
Turkestan
Gobi

Hot deserts
Sahara
Namib/Kalahari
Arabian
Iranian
Atacama
Australian

Sahara

The Sahara is almost one-third the size of Africa, and is nearly as big as the USA, the fourth largest country. It was not always a desert. Over millions of years it has been covered in ice, sea, forests and grasslands.

Moving dunes

Sand dunes move. The wind blows the sand up one side of the dune, and some of the sand trickles over the top and slips down the other side. Dunes creep forward between 10 and 50 m (33 to 164 ft) a year, and can engulf villages and oases.

Temperature

The temperature at night in a hot desert can drop below freezing, to −4°C (24°F). During the day, the sand can be as hot as 79°C (175°F).

Desert snow

Each year, a thin layer of snow (5 cm, 2 in) blankets the cacti in many North American deserts. And snow sometimes falls on the Ahaggar Mountains in the Sahara Desert.

Desert dinosaurs

Dinosaurs once lived in the Gobi Desert in Asia. Fossilized eggs and bones have been found there, and the skeleton of *Tarbosaurus bataar*, a giant tyrannosaur.

The seashore

The coastline of the world

If all the coastlines were straightened out, they would stretch nearly 13 times around the Equator. The total amount of coastline in the world, not counting small bays and inlets, is 504,000 km (313,186 miles).

Stormy weather

On the shores of the northern Pacific Ocean, the force of the waves in winter is equivalent to the impact of a car crashing into a wall at 145 km (90 miles) an hour. Storm waves on the east coast of North America tossed a 61 kg (135 lb) rock 28 m (91 ft) high – on to the roof of a lighthouse.

Rising tide

On the shore, the sea rises and falls twice a day, at high and low tides. The difference between high and low tide levels ranges from 12 m (40 ft) on some British and Alaskan coasts, to only 30 cm (1 ft) on the Gulf of Mexico coast. The greatest tide is in the Bay of Fundy, eastern Canada, which rises an enormous 16 m (53 ft). The Mediterranean Sea barely has a tide at all.

Beach dunes

Sand dunes on the Atlantic coast of France reach an amazing 91 m (300 ft) high, although beach sand dunes are usually no more than 15 m (50 ft) high. The dunes, blown along by the wind, creep slowly inland, by about 6 m (20 ft) a year, and may bury buildings – and even whole forests.

Skeletons galore!

Corals, which grow in warm, tropical waters, are the skeletons of billions of tiny animals. The Great Barrier Reef is made of coral, and stretches in a series of islands and reefs for 2,028 km (1,260 miles) along the north-east coast of Australia. The Reef has taken at least 12 million years to grow.

DID YOU KNOW?

The highest sea cliffs are on the north coast of Moloka'i, Hawaii – a towering 1,005 m (3,300 ft) high. That is about the same height as a 275-storey building.

Sand between the toes

Sand is worn down rock, washed down to the sea by rivers, or made by waves battering and grinding down rocky cliffs. A few beaches have some desert sand, such as those on the Mediterranean Sea, where sand has been blown by the wind across from the Sahara Desert. Some beaches have sand of all one colour, such as the beaches of black lava on Tahiti. Other beaches are a mixture of colours, made from different types of rock, or from worn down coral or seashells. These are some of the sand colours.

Colour	Made of
Black	Lava
Grey	Granite, feldspar
Light brown/tan	Granite, quartz
Yellow	Quartz
Gold	Mica
Red	Garnet
Pink	Feldspar
White	Coral, seashells, quartz

Rock carving

Coastlines are always changing. On rocky shores, the waves pound against the cliffs, flinging up boulders, pebbles and sand. These grind away the rock, forming bays, caves and arches. The top of an arch may collapse, leaving a sea stack, such as the 137 m (450 ft) tall Old Man of Hoy, off the Orkney Islands.

The waves can act as a huge saw, cutting away the softer rock at the foot of a cliff, so that part of the cliff collapses. The lighthouse on the coast at Martha's Vineyard, Massachusetts, USA, has had to be moved 3 times. The waves wear away about 1.7 m (5.5 ft) of the cliff every year.

Mangrove swamps

Enormous mangrove swamps grow in shallow waters on some shores in tropical regions, such as around the mouth of the Ganges River in India. Some mangrove swamps can stretch for 97 km (60 miles) or more inland. The mangrove trees can reach 25 m (82 ft) tall, and have curious stilt-like roots, which prop up the trees.

The changing shore

The level of the sea on the seashore can change over long periods of time. Many of the Ancient Roman ports around the Mediterranean Sea, such as Caesarea on the coast of Israel, are now drowned. In contrast, on Romney Marshes, in Kent, England, the old port of Rye is now over 3 km (2 miles) inland.

The sea

The blue planet

Saltwater covers nearly 70 per cent of the surface of the Earth. The continents and islands divide all that water into the Pacific, Atlantic, Indian and Arctic Oceans – but the four oceans form one continuous expanse of water.

The oceans		
Name	Size, excluding major seas	Average depth
Pacific Ocean	165,384,000 sq km	4,000 m
Atlantic Ocean	82,217,000 sq km	3,300 m
Indian Ocean	73,481,000 sq km	3,800 m
Arctic Ocean	13,986,000 sq km	1,500 m

The largest ocean, the Pacific, covers nearly one-third of the Earth's surface. At its widest point, between Panama and Malaysia, the Pacific stretches 17,700 km (11,000 miles) – nearly halfway around the world.

DID YOU KNOW?

Sound can travel through water at (1,507 in 14,954 ft) a second. That is about 5 times faster than sound travelling through air – 331m (1,087 ft) a second.

Saltwater

Saltwater contains over 96 per cent pure water and nearly 3 per cent common salt. More than 80 other elements, including gold, make up the rest. These nine substances are found in the greatest quantity.

Sulphate Bromide
Magnesium Boron
Calcium Strontium
Potassium Fluoride
Bicarbonate

Drinking the sea

When saltwater freezes, the ice contains little or no salt. People living in polar regions, such as Eskimos, can melt the ice – and use it as fresh drinking water.

Tsunamis

Tsunamis, often wrongly called tidal waves, are huge waves caused either by an underwater volcanic explosion or by an earthquake.

One tsunami, triggered by an earthquake, took just over 4½ hours, to travel a distance of 3,220 km (2,000 miles) – from the Aleutian Trench under the north Pacific to Honolulu, in the mid Pacific. The tsunami hit the island with waves more than 15 m (50 ft) high.

Oceans and seas

Each ocean is divided into different areas – the main part, called by the ocean name, and various seas. The seas are mostly around the coasts of the continents and islands. These are the largest seas in each of the oceans.

Ocean	Name of sea	Size
Pacific	Coral	4,790,000 sq km
	South China	3,680,000 sq km
Atlantic	Caribbean	2,750,000 sq km
	Mediterranean	2,510,000 sq km
Indian	Red	450,000 sq km
	Persian Gulf	240,000 sq km
Arctic	Hudson Bay	1,230,000 sq km
	Baffin Bay	690,000 sq km

Hot and cold water

The surface of the sea varies in temperature. The warm, tropical currents can be as hot as 30°C (86°F), the polar currents can be as cold as −2°C (29°F). In the north Atlantic, where the warm Gulf Stream meets the cold Labrador Current, there is a 12°C (22°F) difference in temperature.

Sailing clockwise

The water in the seas is constantly moving around the Earth, flowing in great currents, like rivers in the sea. The currents may be as wide as 80 km (50 miles) and flow at up to 6 km (4 miles) an hour.

The currents in the southern hemisphere mostly swirl anti-clockwise; those in the northern hemisphere swirl in a clockwise direction. In 1492, Columbus sailed from Spain to the West Indies along two currents, the Canaries and the North Equatorial.

Amazing But True

If all the salt was taken out of the seas and spread over the land surface of the Earth, there would be a layer of salt 152 m (500 ft) thick.

Salty seas

The amount of salt in seawater varies. The Red Sea, in the Near East, has almost six times as much salt as the Baltic Sea, in Europe.

Icelandic warmth

The warm Gulf Stream flows from the Caribbean eastwards across the Atlantic Ocean and on past Iceland as far as northern Europe. The winds blowing across the Gulf Stream keep Reyjavik, in Iceland, warmer in winter than New York City, USA 3,862 km (2,400 miles) further south, where there are winds blowing from the cold Labrador Current.

Under the sea

The ocean floor

The ocean floor is not completely flat – there are volcanoes, mountains, valleys and plains, just as there are on dry land.

The ocean plains are solid rock, covered in places in a layer of sand, gravel, clay, silt, or ooze – the remains of countless billions of sea creatures. On average, the layer is 30 m (100 ft) thick; on the floor of the Mediterranean Sea, it is 2,000 m (6,500 ft) thick.

DID YOU KNOW?

The deeper under the sea you go, the greater the pressure, that is the weight of the water above you. At a depth of 9,100 m (30,000 ft), the pressure is equivalent to a 1 tonne weight balanced on a postage stamp.

Undersea mountains

There are mountains in every ocean – together, they form a chain over 60,000 km (37,284 miles) long. In the Pacific Ocean alone there are 14,000 sea mountains, their peaks 610-1,829 m (2,000-6,000 ft) below the surface. Other sea mountains are so huge, they poke through the surface as chains of islands. This map shows the underwater mountain chains.

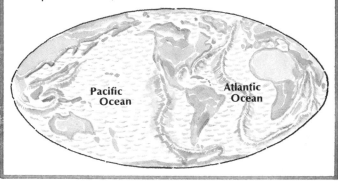

Flashlight fish

Many fish living 3,000 m (9,842 ft) down in the dark ocean waters, have their own lights, which are made by bacteria inside the fish. The bacteria glow all the time, but the fish can "switch" the lights off and on.

The angler fish has a bulb of bacteria light at the end of a long spine, which hangs over the fish's mouth. The light attracts other fish – which are gobbled up by the angler.

Light and dark

In the muddy waters off the shores, the water is clear for only about 15 m (50 ft) down. Out in the open ocean, it is clear down to about 110 m (360 ft), and some sunlight can reach 244 m (800 ft) deep. Below that level, it is dark, still – and cold. Deep water is about 3.8°C (39°F), which is close to freezing all the year round.

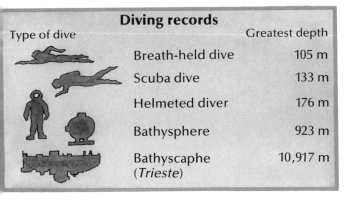

Diving records

Type of dive		Greatest depth
	Breath-held dive	105 m
	Scuba dive	133 m
	Helmeted diver	176 m
	Bathysphere	923 m
	Bathyscaphe (*Trieste*)	10,917 m

Deepest dive

Explorers, inside the bathyscaphe *Trieste*, have dived almost to the bottom of the Mariana Trench, the deepest point on Earth. The Trench, south-west of Guam in the Pacific Ocean, plunges to a depth of 11,033 m (36,198 ft) below sea level.

Fishy depths

Different plants and animals live at different depths in the oceans. Floating on the surface, mostly around the coasts and in tropical seas, are billions of tiny plants and animals, called plankton.

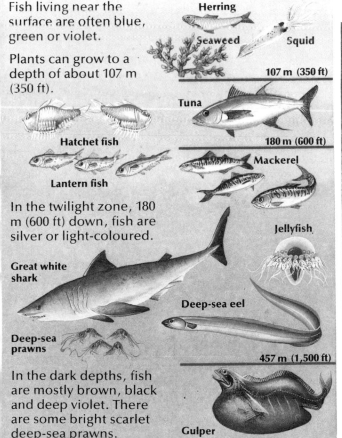

Fish living near the surface are often blue, green or violet.

Plants can grow to a depth of about 107 m (350 ft).

Herring

Seaweed

Squid

107 m (350 ft)

Hatchet fish

Tuna

180 m (600 ft)

Lantern fish

Mackerel

In the twilight zone, 180 m (600 ft) down, fish are silver or light-coloured.

Jellyfish

Great white shark

Deep-sea eel

Deep-sea prawns

457 m (1,500 ft)

In the dark depths, fish are mostly brown, black and deep violet. There are some bright scarlet deep-sea prawns.

Gulper

Amazing But True

Huge worms, 3 m (10 ft) long, blind crabs and giant white clams survive 2,400 m (8,000 ft) down in the darkness of the Pacific Ocean, off the coast of South America. They live near a crack in the ocean floor, where hot mineral-rich water gushes out, providing them with food.

Poles apart

The Arctic Ocean

The Arctic is the smallest of the four oceans, and is less than one-tenth the size of the Pacific, the largest ocean.

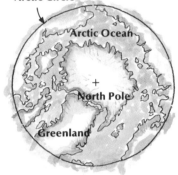

Greenland ice sheet statistics	
Area of ice sheet	1,479,000 sq km
Volume of ice	2,800,000 cu km
Thickness of ice	1.6-3 km
Temperature	
July	over 10°C
December	−50°C
Average	−20°C

Arctic Ocean statistics	
Total area	13,986,000 sq km
Area of floating ice	12,000,000 sq km
Average depth of water	1,500 m
Thickness of pack ice	0.6-7.43 m
Coldest water temperature	−51°C

Greenland

About 85 per cent of Greenland is covered by an ice sheet, stretching 2,400 km (1,491 miles) from north to south and up to 1,100 km (683 miles) east to west. The ice sheet is 7½ times the size of Britain. The 50,000 people on the island can only live on the coasts.

Slow-growing plants

Some Arctic lichens may be over 4,500 years old, and have taken hundreds of years to grow 2.5 cm (1 in).

All that ice

The polar ice sheets hold just over 2 per cent of all the Earth's water. If all the ice melted, the sea level around the world would rise by about 60 m (200 ft). Many coastal areas would be drowned, including major cities such as London, Tokyo and New York.

Hunt the seal

In the Arctic, seals spend much of their time under water, but need to come up for air about every 20 minutes. When the seas are frozen, the seals chew several big breathing holes in the ice.

Polar bears hunt seals, and wait on the ice by a breathing hole. When the seal comes up, the polar bear grabs it.

Midnight Sun

As the Earth travels around the Sun, one of the Poles is always facing towards it. The North Pole has continuous daylight from mid-March to mid-September. From mid-September to mid-March, it is the South Pole's turn for continuous daylight.

Antarctica

Nearly one-tenth of the Earth's surface is permanently covered in ice. About 90 per cent of all that ice is in the ice sheets of Antarctica and Greenland. The other 10 per cent is in mountain glaciers.

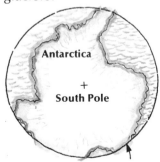

The Antarctic ice sheet is 1½ times the size of the USA, and has nine times more ice than the Greenland ice sheet.

Antarctic wildlife

Insects, 13 mm (0.5 in) long, are the only creatures living all the time on Antarctica itself. The wildlife lives in the seas and islands around the coast, including the blue whale, the largest creature on Earth, 30 m (98 ft) long and 136 tonnes in weight.

Penguins live on the islands. Scientists think that Adelie penguins might use the Sun to navigate back to their nests from up to 3,058 km (1,900 miles) away. Penguins can "fly" underwater at 40 km (25 miles) an hour.

DID YOU KNOW?

There is no land at the North Pole – it is a floating raft of ice. In 1958, *Nautilus*, the US submarine, was the first to cross the Arctic Ocean – a distance of 2,945 km (1,830 miles) – by travelling underneath the North Pole.

Volcano

There is still one active volcano in Antarctica. Mount Erebus, in the Transantarctic Range, reaches up 4,900 m (16,075 ft) above the ice. Erebus steams and spouts ash, even though it is covered in snow.

Antarctica statistics	
Area of ice sheet	13,000,000 sq km
Volume of ice sheet	29,000,000 cu km
Thickness of ice	3-4 km
Area of sea ice	
March	3,000,000 sq km
September	22,000,000 sq km
Average thickness of sea ice	4 m
Temperature	
Interior average	−50°C
Coastal average	−20°C

Icebergs and glaciers

Icing

Glaciers cover 10½ per cent of the Earth's land surface, an area equal to the size of South America. Glaciers contain enough ice to cover the entire Earth with a layer of ice, 30 m (98 ft) thick.

Glacier lengths		
Name	Location	Length
Lambert/Fisher Ice Passage	Antarctica	515 km
Novaya Zemlya Glacier	USSR	418 km
Arctic Institute Ice Passage	Antarctica	362 km
Nimrod/Lennox/King Ice Passage	Antarctica	289 km
Denman Glacier	Antarctica	241 km
Beardmore Glacier	Antarctica	225 km
Recovery Glacier	Antarctica	225 km
Petermanns Gletscher Glacier	Greenland	200 km
Unnamed Glacier	Antarctica	193 km

Glaciers on the move

Glaciers creep down mountains at a rate of between 2.5-60 cm (1-24 in) a day. A few glaciers move much faster, such as two on Greenland: up to 24 m (79 ft) a day for the Quarayag Glacier and 28 m (92 ft) for the Rinks Isbrae Glacier.

Busy glacier

The Jakobshavn Isbrae Glacier in Greenland moves at about 7 km (4 miles) a year. Every day, over 142 million tonnes of ice break off and float away as 1,500 or so icebergs each year.

DID YOU KNOW?

At least 75 per cent of all the freshwater on Earth is deep frozen inside glaciers. That amount of water would equal non-stop rain all over the Earth for as much as 60 years.

Tropical glaciers

Glaciers and snowfields are found near the Equator, on mountains which are over 6,000 m (20,000 ft) high. There is glacier ice 61 m (200 ft) deep in the Kibo Peak crater on Mount Kilimanjaro in Tanzania.

Deep ice

A depth of glacier ice as thick as 4,330 m (14,206 ft) has been recorded on Byrd Station in Antarctica. Most glaciers are between 91-3,000 m (299-9,842 ft) deep.

Crevasse

Crevasses, cracks in glaciers, can be 40 m (131 ft) deep. The bodies of climbers who fell into a crevasse in the Bossons Glacier on Mont Blanc in the Alps in 1820, were not found until 1861, when they reached the melting "snout", the end of the glacier.

Amazing But True

An Arctic iceberg drifted about 4,000 km (2,486 miles), nearly as far south as the island of Bermuda. An Antarctic iceberg drifted about 5,500 km (3,418 miles), nearly as far north as Rio de Janeiro, in Brazil.

Biggest berg

The largest iceberg ever recorded, off the coast of Antarctica, was 335 km (208 miles) long and 97 km (60 miles) wide. It covered an area of 31,000 sq km (12,000 sq miles), about the same size as Belgium.

Hidden depth

Only about one-tenth of an iceberg floats above the surface. If there is 122 m (400 ft) above the water, then there must be as much as 1,098 m (3,600 ft) below the water.

Icy heights

The tallest iceberg ever recorded, off west Greenland, was 167 m (550 ft) high. That is more than half as tall as the Eiffel Tower in Paris, France.

Iceberg ahoy!

The International Ice Patrol keeps track of all icebergs, and warns ships of any possible danger. The Patrol was set up after the giant liner, the *Titanic,* sank after hitting an iceberg on the night of 14 April 1912: 1,490 people drowned out of a total of 2,201 passengers and crew.

Watering the desert

Icebergs are made of freshwater and could be used to supply water in desert areas. Scientists think that tugs could be built, which could tow large icebergs at a rate of 400 km (250 miles) a day.

The journey from Antarctica to western Australia might take 107-150 days, and to the Atacama Desert in Chile 145-200 days. Only about half of each iceberg would melt on the way.

Long-life bergs

Satellites can track the lives of icebergs. The Trolltunga iceberg in Antarctica was tracked for 11 years, until it broke up into several smaller bergs. At up to 25 km (15½ miles) a day, icebergs can travel a total distance of as much as 2,500 km (1,550 miles).

Earthquakes

Earthquake areas

Earthquakes happen under the sea as well as on land. Ninety per cent occur in the "ring of fire", which circles the Pacific Ocean. Many others occur along the Alpine Belt, which stretches from Spain to Turkey, and on through the Himalayas as far as South-East Asia.

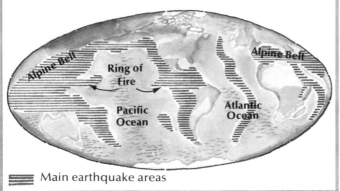

Main earthquake areas

Disaster area

China, on the Alpine Belt of earthquakes, has the worst record for earthquake deaths. In 1556, an earthquake killed 830,000 people in Shanxi province. In 1976, the earthquake in Tangshan province – 8.2 on the Richter Scale – killed 750,000 people.

Danger!

Magnitude

The magnitude, that is the power, of an earthquake is measured on the Richter Scale. Starting at 1, each number on the Scale is ten times more powerful than the number below. An earthquake of magnitude 7 is about as powerful as a one megaton nuclear bomb; the worst earthquake so far recorded was 8.9.

A million earthquakes

There are about a million earthquakes every year – any vibration of the Earth's crust is an earthquake. Most are so tiny, they only register on a seismograph, which measures the slightest movement in the crust. A large earthquake occurs about every two weeks – mostly under the sea, where it does little harm.

Animals, such as dogs and chickens, some people believe, can sense faint vibrations or smells and warn people that an earthquake might happen. In 1975, in Haicheng, China, thousands of people escaped an earthquake because they were warned of the danger.

DID YOU KNOW?

Earthquakes under the sea can trigger off great avalanches of mud and sand. These can cause undersea currents strong enough to snap underwater cables. Telephone cables broke under the Atlantic Ocean, after the earthquake off Newfoundland in 1929.

Splash!

The shock of an earthquake can sometimes be felt hundreds of kilometres away. Water splashed in swimming pools in Houston, USA, after the earthquake in Mexico in 1985 – 1,609 km (1,000 miles) away.

Shocking

An earthquake usually lasts for less than 1 minute. The earthquake in Lisbon, Portugal, in 1755 lasted for 10 minutes, and the shock waves were felt as far away as North Africa.

Rock avalanches

The 1970 earthquake off the coast of Peru caused an avalanche of snow and rock on land – high on the Nevados Huascaran mountain. The avalanche fell 4,000 m (13,123 ft), and buried the town of Yungay under 10 m (33 ft) of rock, killing at least 18,000 people.

Fire! fire!

Huge fires can break out after an earthquake. In 1906, after the earthquake in San Francisco, USA, fire destroyed the wooden buildings of the city. The water pipes had burst, and the fire raged for 3½ days. But within 9 years, the city had been rebuilt.

Amazing But True

The ground can roll like waves on the ocean in a very bad earthquake. The 1964 earthquake in Alaska lasted for 7 minutes. The shaking opened up huge cracks in the ground, up to 90 cm (3 ft) wide and 12 m (40 ft) deep. Many buildings tilted and slid down into the cracks.

Twentieth-century earthquakes

These are some of the most serious earthquakes this century, measured on the Richter Scale.

Date	Location	Richter Scale
1906	Coast of Colombia	8.9
1906	Jammu and Kashmir, India	8.6
1906	Valparaiso, Chile	8.6
1920	Kansu province, China	8.5
1929	Fox Islands, Alaska	8.6
1933	North Honshu, Japan	8.9
1941	Coast of Portugal	8.4
1950	Assam, India	8.3
1960	Lebu, Chile	8.5
1964	Prince William Sound, Alaska	8.5

Volcanoes

Hot spots

There are more than 600 active volcanoes on Earth. About half of these are in the "ring of fire" – on land and under the sea – which circles the Pacific Ocean;

Indonesia alone has about 160 active volcanoes. Many islands are volcanic, such as the Hawaiian islands – and Iceland, which has about 200 active volcanoes.

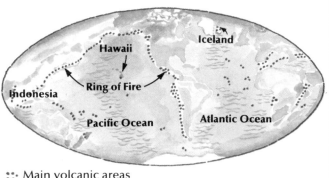

Iceland

Hawaii

Ring of Fire

Indonesia

Pacific Ocean

Atlantic Ocean

∴ Main volcanic areas

Living dangerously

A blanket of ash can cover the countryside when a volcano explodes. But the ash helps make the soil very fertile, and many people risk the danger of living near an active volcano. Three crops of rice a year can be grown on the slopes of Gunung Agung, in Bali, a volcano which exploded in 1963, killing 2,000 people.

Eruptions

On average, between 20-30 volcanoes erupt each year. A few volcanoes erupt more or less all the time, such as the island of Stromboli, Italy, which shoots a shower of glowing ash into the sky every 20 minutes or so. Other volcanoes are dormant; sometimes they do not erupt for tens or hundreds of years. Mount Etna, in Sicily, has erupted about 150 times in the last 3,500 years.

Rivers of fire

Lava is fiery hot molten rock – up to 1200°C (2190°F). On Mount Tolbachik, in the Kamchatka Peninsula, USSR, in 1975, the lava flow gushed out at 168 m (550 ft) a second. And when Laki, in Iceland, exploded in 1782, the hot lava flowed a distance of about 65 km (40 miles).

Hot water

Underground water is heated by the hot rocks in volcanic areas. The water can bubble to the surface as a hot spring, or can spout high in the air as a geyser – a jet of steam and scalding water. Yellowstone Park in the USA has hot springs and 10,000 geysers; Old Faithful Geyser erupts 40 m (130 ft) high every 30-90 minutes.

Glowing clouds

Volcanoes can release clouds of ash, as well as cinders, gases and lava. Ash clouds can flow downhill at 200 km (124 miles) an hour, or can billow upwards. When Mayon, in the Philippines, erupted in 1968, ash and blocks of lava were hurled 600 m (1,968 ft) into the air, and the ash clouds rose to a height of 10 km (6 miles).

Major active volcanoes by continent			
Continent	Country	Volcano	Height
Asia	USSR	Kluchevskaya	4,750 m
Africa	Zaire	Nyiragongo	3,520 m
North America	Alaska	My Wrangell	4,270 m
South America	Argentina	Antofalla	6,127 m
Antarctica	Ross Island	Erebus	3,720 m
Europe	Sicily	Etna	3,340 m
Oceania	New Zealand	Ruapehu	2,797 m

Mud avalanches

Some volcanic explosions trigger off a lethal avalanche of mud. When the Nevado del Ruiz, in Colombia, erupted in 1985, the heat melted the ice and snow on the peak. This caused a torrent of mud and water, which destroyed the town of Armero in five minutes, killing 20,000 people.

DID YOU KNOW?

The largest active volcano on Earth is Mauna Loa, in Hawaii. It is 4,168 m (13,677 ft) high, and one eruption lasted for 1½ years.

Lava tubes

Lava flows can be 20 m (66 ft) thick, and can take several years to cool. Inside some flows are huge tunnels – lava tubes, as much as 10 m (33 ft) high. Hot lava hangs down from the tube roof as lava stalactites, and drips on to the tube floor, forming lava stalagmites.

Krakatoa

The loudest sound ever recorded was the eruption which blew up the island of Krakatoa, near Java, in 1883. The noise was heard in Australia, 4,800 km (3,000 miles) away, and the shock was felt in California, USA, 14,500 km (9,000 miles) away.

Rock and fire blasted 80 km (50 miles) up into the air. The wind carried volcanic dust around the Earth, causing vivid sunsets as far away as London, England. Tsunamis, huge waves 30 m (100 ft) high, crashed 16 km (10 miles) inland on Java and Sumatra, killing 36,000 people.

Natural resources

What are natural resources?

Many resources from the Earth provide light and heat, such as oil, coal and gas from under the ground, and firewood and charcoal from trees. And hot water and steam can be piped up from under the ground.

The power of the water in rivers, and the speed of the wind, are used to generate electricity. And sunlight is collected in solar panels and cells, to heat water and supply electricity.

Will natural resources last forever?

The supply of fossil fuels, that is oil, coal and gas, which were formed millions of years ago, will run out one day. At the rate we are burning them at present, scientists think that oil and gas may be used up in 70 years' time, and coal in 300 years' time. But there may be more supplies in the ground and under the sea which have not yet been found.

Oil rig

Twenty per cent of the world's oil comes from wells beneath the sea. One North Sea oil rig can produce up to 320,000 litres (70,400 gallons) of oil a day. At an average of 55 litres (12 gallons) each, that would fill the petrol tanks of 5,800 cars.

Coal supply

Coal was mined by the Romans as long ago as the 1st century AD. But there is still a huge amount of coal in the ground. These countries have the biggest reserves of coal.

USSR   UK
USA   Poland
China   Australia
West Germany

DID YOU KNOW?

Only 5.5 per cent of the world's population live in the USA. But they use nearly 29 per cent of the world's petrol and nearly 33 per cent of the world's electricity.

Sources of energy

These are the major natural resources that are used for energy on Earth today.

Source of energy		Per cent
🌢🌢🌢🌢🌢	Oil	39
🪨🪨🪨🪨🪨	Coal	27
💧💧💧💧💧	Gas	17
🌳🌳🌳🌳	Fuelwood/charcoal	12
🌊🌊🌊	Hydro (water) power	2
♨️♨️♨️♨️	Other, such as underground heat and hot water springs	2
🏭🏭🏭🏭	Nuclear power	1

River power

The force of flowing water in rivers and over waterfalls is used to generate nearly one-quarter of the world's electricity. These are some of the countries using water power to make their electricity.

Country	Per cent
Norway	100
Brazil	93
Switzerland	79
Canada	70
France	50
Italy	50
Japan	30
West Germany	20
USA	20
USSR	20

Boiling water

Hot water is piped from under the ground in Iceland, and used to heat homes, factories – and outdoor swimming pools. The capital city, Reykjavik, is supplied with 250 litres (55 gallons) of boiling water every second.

Products from fossil fuels

Many products are made from coal and oil. These are just a few examples.

Products from coal

Plastics
Heavy chemicals
Perfumes
Insectides
Antiseptics
Road surfaces
Coal gas

Products from oil

Petrol (gasoline)
Kerosene (jet fuel)
Diesel fuel
Paraffin wax
Pharmaceuticals
Explosives
Pesticides
Detergents
Cosmetics
Adhesives
Polishes
Paints
Nylon
Plastics

Using the Sun

Solar panels in the roofs of houses trap the heat from the Sun. Many homes in Israel, Canada, Australia and Japan have solar panels. Panels covering as little as 3 sq m (32 sq ft) can heat as much as 226 litres (50 gallons) of water a day – enough for 2 baths and all the washing up.

Rocks, minerals and metals

The rocks of the Earth's crust

The Earth's crust is made up of different kinds of rocks. They all belong to one of the 3 rock families, which are called igneous, sedimentary and metamorphic. These are some examples of the different families.

Igneous rocks

Igneous rocks are made from hot, molten rock, deep inside the Earth's mantle.

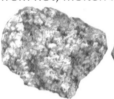

Granite
Hard, coarse-grained rock

Basalt
Hard, fine-grained rock

Obsidian
Black or greenish volcanic glass

Sedimentary rocks

Sedimentary rocks are layers made from worn fragments of rock, and may contain the remains of plants and animals.

Limestone
Hard rock; often contains lots of shells

Chalk
Soft rock; contains remains of small animals and shells

Sandstone
Formed from beach, river or desert sands

Metamorphic rocks

Metamorphic rocks are made from rocks which are pushed back down in the mantle, where they change under heat and pressure into different rocks.

Slate
Formed under high pressure from shale

Marble
Formed under heat from different limestones

Quartzite
Formed under heat and high pressure from sandstone

Minerals

The rocks of the Earth's crust contain a mixture of over 2,000 minerals. But about 90 per cent of the crust is made up of just 20 minerals, such as mica, quartz and feldspar. These are the uses of some minerals.

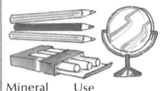

Mineral	Use
Graphite	Lead pencil
Gypsum	School chalk
Silica	Glass, mirrors
Potassium	Fertilizers
Sodium	
Fluorite	Toothpaste
Cobalt	Blue colouring
Sodium chloride	Household salt

Amazing But True

Pumice, a kind of lava, is full of gas bubbles, and is light enough to float on water – the only rock to do so.

Elementary!

Rocks are a mixture of one or more minerals. Minerals are made up of chemical elements. These are the chemical elements found in the greatest quantity in the Earth's crust.

Name of element	Per cent
Oxygen	46.60
Silicon	27.72
Aluminium	8.13
Iron	5.00
Calcium	3.63
Sodium	2.82
Potassium	2.59
Magnesium	2.09 = 98.6%
Titanium	0.44
Hydrogen	0.14
Phosphorus	0.12
Manganese	0.10
Fluorine	0.08
Sulphur	0.05
Chlorine	0.04
Carbon	0.03 = 1.0%
Others, including gold and silver	0.41 = 0.4%

Sparklers

About 100 minerals, because of their beauty and rarity, are known as gemstones, such as diamonds and sapphires. Emeralds and rubies are the most valuable gems; they are the rarest.

DID YOU KNOW?

Minerals are graded according to their hardness, on a scale from 1 to 10. Talc, used as talcum powder, is the softest mineral, rated 1; quartz rates 7. Diamond is rated 10 – the hardest mineral on Earth. Only a diamond can be used to cut and polish another diamond.

Diamond bright

Diamonds are found in a rainbow of colours – white, yellow, pink, green, blue, brown, red and black. In the ground, they usually look like dull, rounded pebbles – they only glitter and shine once they have been cut and polished. The small and badly-coloured diamonds are used in cutting tools.

Metalwork

Many of the metals in the rocks of the Earth's crust, such as silver, tin, mercury, iron and lead, have been mined for thousands of years. In the Middle East, 8,000 years ago, copper and gold were used for making jewellery. The gold mask of the Pharaoh Tutankhamun was made over 3,000 years ago.

Gold diggers

Miners today have to dig as much as 2 tonnes (2 tons) of rock to find only 28 grams (1 oz) of gold. If the 50 million tonnes of waste rock from just one South African gold mine were spread out, the rock would bury Manhattan island, New York, USA, under a layer 2.4 m (8 ft) deep.

Changing the world

The people on Earth

The Earth has a limited amount of oil and coal, wood and soil. People are using up these natural resources at an alarming rate, as well as spoiling the landscape and polluting the water and air – and may be changing the future of the Earth.

Croplands

Trees and hedges have been dug up to make enormous fields. One cornfield in the American Midwest can be 810 hectares (2,000 acres) in size. This makes harvesting the crops easier. But growing the same crop every year makes the soil less fertile and the harvest becomes smaller each year. And pests can destroy whole fields of crops.

Deserts

The deserts of the world are growing bigger, taking over the farmland at the edges, because of creeping sand dunes. The Sahara Desert alone is expanding southwards at an average of 0.8 km (½ mile) a month.

Water pollution

Chemical waste from factories is dumped or washed into seas, lakes and rivers, where it kills fish and plants. The Mediterranean Sea is one of the most polluted areas of water on Earth. In some places, the surface is now covered with a thin film of oil spilled from ships, and it is not safe to swim.

The changing climate

Some scientists think that burning coal and oil, and burning tropical forests, might lead to a change in the weather – the Earth might grow warmer, by as much as 7°C (12.5°F) at the Poles. This would melt some of the ice, and sea levels could rise by up to 7 m (23 ft), drowning all the ports.

Other scientists think that the dust produced by burning coal, oil and wood could block out some of the Sun's rays. The Earth might become colder – great sheets of ice could cover the northern hemisphere at least as far south as London, England.

Farmland

Only 11 per cent of the Earth's land is used for farming. But each year, less and less land can be used for growing crops and grazing cattle because the soil is washed away by the rain or blown away by the wind.

In the 1930s, farmers in the American Southwest ploughed up the plains to grow wheat. But as much as 25 cm (10 in) of soil was blown away by the wind – creating the Dust Bowl, where no plants could grow.

DID YOU KNOW?

Every year, the amount of trees cut down could cover a city the size of Birmingham, England, with a pile of wood, ten storeys high.

Vanishing forest

Forests cover just over a quarter of the Earth. But every year, forests the size of England, Scotland and Wales are cut down or spoilt. By the year 2000, one-third of all the tropical forests may have been destroyed.

Too much traffic

The exhaust fumes from cars, buses and trucks can poison the air. More than one-third of West Germany's Black Forest is dying, probably from the effect of these fumes. Cities, such as Los Angeles, USA and Tokyo, Japan, are often covered with a thick, choking smog. This is caused by the reaction of exhaust fumes and sunlight.

Acid rain

Factories and power stations burning oil and coal put huge amounts of poisonous gases and chemicals into the air. These combine with rain and snow and can fall hundreds of kilometres away, destroying forests and killing all the life in lakes.

Carried by the wind, pollution from British factories has killed many of the fish and plants in 18,000 lakes in Sweden. And more than half the pollution which falls on Canada comes from the USA.

Mining

Mining for minerals, such as bauxite, can destroy vast areas of land, and can cause pollution. Waste from copper mining in Malaysia has been washed into rivers, poisoning the fish.

The Earth's future

The people on Earth

Over the centuries, people have made great changes to the Earth – many of them bad. But people are now trying to do something to look after the soil, recycle rubbish and help stop some of the air and water pollution.

Cleaning up

Polluted lakes and rivers can be cleaned up. Filters fitted to power stations can remove some of the gases pouring into the air, or some of the gases can be treated and turned into fertilizer. Fish now swim in the River Thames, once one of the most polluted rivers in Europe, because factory wastes are treated and not dumped in the river.

Terracing

Heavy rain can wash the soil away on steep mountain slopes. Building terraces holds back the soil, and crops can be grown. There are terraces in Bali, where three crops of rice can be grown each year.

Pest control

In parts of China, ducks are used instead of pesticides to control insect pests in rice fields. In the Big Sand commune, thousands of ducks eat about 200 insects each an hour. This system has another advantage, because rain can wash the pesticide off the fields into lakes and rivers, where it pollutes the water.

Saving water

Spraying crops with water in dry areas is very wasteful because so much is lost in evaporation. Huge amounts of water can be saved by giving plants small measured amounts of water, through holes in thin plastic tubes. In Israel, computers control when to turn the water off and on and when to give the plants fertilizer.

Looking after the soil

The soil can be made more fertile by growing different crops together, rather than growing only one crop. In Java, pineapples and winged beans are grown in alternate rows, which keeps the soil fertile.

Tree planting

More trees are being planted, to supply wood for industry, and fuel for heating and cooking. In South Korea, where most of the wood is used for fuel, 70 per cent of the country has now been planted with young trees. And in Gujarat, India, school children are planting tree seedlings, to provide wood for heating and cooking.

Recycling rubbish

Rubbish can be sorted and recycled. Over half the aluminium drinks cans in the USA are melted down and recycled. In Britain, glass bottles are sorted into different colours, melted and reused.

Planting the desert

Expanding deserts can be stopped by planting bushes at the edges to hold back the sand dunes. And the bushes can be used for crops too – jojoba produces liquid wax, and guayule and a type of dandelion can produce latex, which is used as rubber.

Farming the wind

Electricity can be generated by windmills – rather than by power stations which burn oil or coal. Fields full of windmills could supply 8 per cent of electricity in California, USA by the year 2000. A wind "farm", with about 4,600 windmills, can supply as many as 30,000 homes with electricity.

Saving coal and oil

Using rubbish for fuel saves oil or coal. In Edmonton, England, electricity is generated by burning about 2 per cent of Britain's total rubbish, saving about 100,000 tonnes of coal each year.

Saving trees

About 35 million trees could be saved each year, if 75 per cent of waste paper and cardboard was recycled into pulp and used to make new paper.

DID YOU KNOW?

A quarter of all the cars in Brazil run on fuel made from sugar cane, and half the cars in South Africa use fuel made from liquid coal.

Earth map

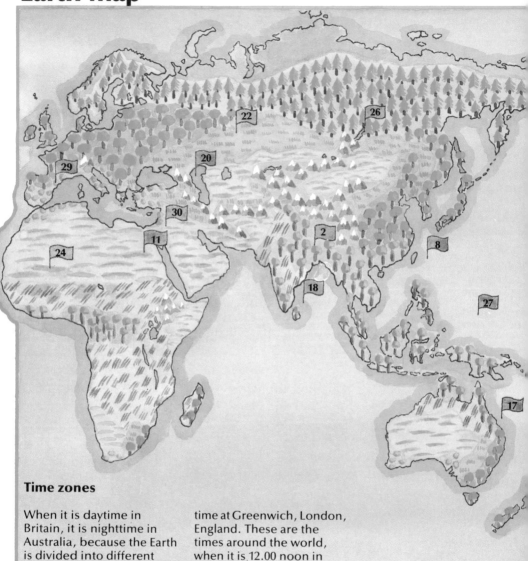

Time zones

When it is daytime in Britain, it is nighttime in Australia, because the Earth is divided into different time zones – based on the time at Greenwich, London, England. These are the times around the world, when it is 12.00 noon in London.

London, England

Moscow, USSR

Dacca, Bangladesh

Tokyo, Japan

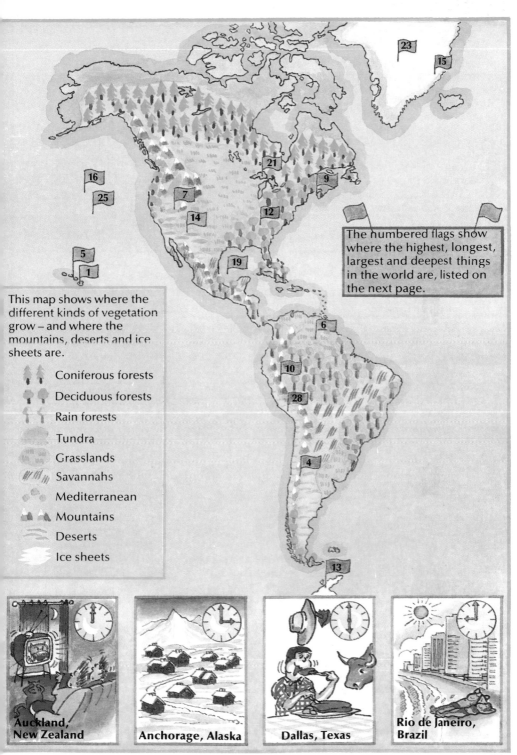

This map shows where the different kinds of vegetation grow – and where the mountains, deserts and ice sheets are.

Coniferous forests
Deciduous forests
Rain forests
Tundra
Grasslands
Savannahs
Mediterranean
Mountains
Deserts
Ice sheets

The numbered flags show where the highest, longest, largest and deepest things in the world are, listed on the next page.

Auckland, New Zealand

Anchorage, Alaska

Dallas, Texas

Rio de Janeiro, Brazil

For key to numbers on map, see next page.

45

The Earth in a nutshell

The highest . . .

1 Mountain on Earth
Mauna Kea, Hawaii
10,023 m measured from
the sea floor

2 Mountain on land
Mount Everest, Nepal/Tibet
8,843 m

3 Mountain under the sea
Near Tonga Trench, Tonga
Islands, Pacific Ocean
8,690 m

4 Active volcano
Antofalla, Argentina
6,127 m

5 Sea cliffs
Umilehi Point, Moloka'i,
Hawaii
1,005 m

6 Waterfall
Angel Falls, Venezuela
979 m

7 Active geyser
Service Steamboat Geyser,
Yellowstone, USA
Maximum 115 m

8 Tsunami
Ishigaki Island, Japan
85 m

9 Tide
Bay of Fundy, Nova Scotia,
Canada
Range of 14.5 m

The longest . . .

10 Mountain range
Andes, South America
7,240 km

11 River
River Nile, Egypt
6,670 km

12 Cave system
Mammoth Cave National
Park, Kentucky, USA
484 km

13 Glacier
Lambert/Mellor, Antarctica
402 km

14 Canyon
Grand Canyon on Colorado
River, Arizona, USA
349 km

15 Fjord
Nordvest Fjord, Greenland
313 km

The largest . . .

16 Ocean
Pacific Ocean
165,384,000 sq km

17 Sea
Coral Sea (part of Pacific
Ocean)
4,790,000 sq km

18 Bay
Bay of Bengal
2,172,000 sq km

19 Gulf
Gulf of Mexico
1,544,000 sq km

20 Inland sea
Caspian Sea, Iran/USSR
372,000 sq km

21 Lake
Lake Superior, Canada/USA
82,414 sq km

22 Continent
Asia
44,391,200 sq km

23 Island
Greenland
2,175,000 sq km

24 Desert
Sahara Desert, North Africa
8,400,000 sq km

The deepest . . .

25 Ocean
Pacific Ocean
Average depth 4,000 m

26 Lake
Lake Baikal, USSR
Maximum 1,940 m

27 Sea trench
Mariana Trench, Pacific
Ocean
11,033 m

28 Canyon
Colca Canyon, Peru
3,223 m

29 Cave
Gouffre Jean Bernard,
France
1,535 m

30 Land below sea level
Dead Sea, Israel/Jordan
395 m

The numbered flags on pages 44-45 show where these places are.

Index

COUNTRIES
OF THE WORLD
FACTS

Neil Champion

CONTENTS

Designed by Stephen Meir, Joe Coonan, Anil Dumasia and Tony Gibson

**Illustrated by Tony Gibson
Additional illustrations by Mario Saporito, Ian Jackson and Chris Lyon**

Researched by Margaret Harvey

Country facts

The 5 largest countries
(square kilometres)

USSR	22,402,000
Canada	9,976,000
China	9,597,000
USA	9,363,000
Brazil	8,512,000

The 5 smallest countries
(square kilometres)

Vatican City	0.4
Monaco	2
Nauru	21
Tuvalu	26
San Marino	61

The largest island

Greenland is the largest island. It is almost 10 times larger than Britain but only 50,000 people live there. This means that if all the people were spread out evenly, each one would have 10,000 times as much room as each person living in Britain.

Longest coastline

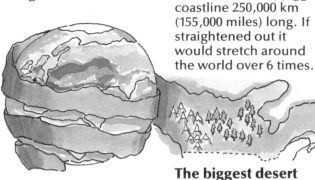

Canada has a very jagged coastline 250,000 km (155,000 miles) long. If straightened out it would stretch around the world over 6 times.

Oldest and newest

The oldest country is Iran (or Persia as it used to be known). It has been an independent country since the 6th century BC. The newest country is Brunei, which became independent of Britain in 1984.

The biggest desert

The world's largest desert is the Sahara. It covers part or all of 10 northern and west African countries, including Chad, Niger, Libya, Algeria, Egypt, Mali and Mauritania. It is larger than Australia, the world's sixth largest country. A person left in the desert with no water or shade would die in a day. The temperature can reach 50°C (122°F).

DID YOU KNOW?

The Vatican City, the smallest country in the world, has a population the size of a small village – 1,000 people. One hundred of these are Swiss Guards; their uniforms were designed by Michelangelo in the 15th century.

Amazing But True

Antarctica contains 70 per cent of the world's fresh water in the form of ice. In 1958 one iceberg was spotted that was thought to be the size of Belgium. Antarctica has large deposits of minerals, oil and natural gas, but it is not officially owned by any country.

The largest lake

Lake Superior in Canada is the largest lake in the world. If it were drained of all its water, the land reclaimed would cover an area twice the size of the Netherlands.

Mixed country

Yugoslavia has 2 alphabets (Roman and Cyrillic), 3 religions (Roman Catholic, Eastern Orthodox and Islamic), 4 languages (Macedonian, Serb, Croat, and Slovene), 5 nationalities and 6 republics.

Without a coast

There are 26 countries in the world that do not have a coastline. Switzerland is one of these, but it has a merchant navy.

Busy frontier

More than 120 million people cross the border between Mexico and the USA every year, making it the busiest frontier. The least busy frontier is between East and West Germany, called the Berlin Wall, where only about 200 people cross each year.

How many countries?

There are now 171 independent countries, whereas in 1900 there were only 53. There are also 56 territories, which were once countries but are not now independent.

DID YOU KNOW?

China has the greatest number of frontiers. It rubs shoulders with 13 other countries.

N. Korea	1.	Laos	10.
USSR	2. 2a.	Vietnam	11.
Mongolia	3.	Macau	12.
Afghanistan	4.	Hong Kong	13.
Pakistan	5.		
India	6. 6a. 6b.		
Nepal	7.		
Bhutan	8.		
Burma	9.		

Country of islands

Indonesia is made up of over 13,000 islands, together covering about 2 million sq km (770,000 sq miles). This is equal to the area of Mexico.

51

Populations

Largest populations

China	1,042,000,000
India	762,000,000
USSR	278,000,000
USA	239,000,000
Indonesia	170,000,000

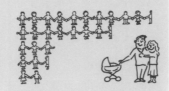

Population density

Although Australia has a population 3 times larger than Hong Kong, it is 8,000 times larger in area. If the people were spread out evenly over the land each Australian would have 500,000 sq m compared with only 200 sq metres for each person in Hong Kong.

Age distribution

In Africa almost half the population is under 15 years old and only 3 out of 100 can expect to live to 65. In Europe the opposite is true. Only one fifth of the population is under 15 and 12 in every 100 live to be 65.

DID YOU KNOW?

The population of New York, the largest city in the USA, is only about 3 per cent of the entire population. But 20 per cent, or 1 in 5, Mexicans live in their biggest city, Mexico City.

Life expectations

Men and women live to an average age of 77 years in Iceland and to an average age of 76 in both Sweden and Japan. In North Yemen and Ethiopia people can expect to live about 40 years.

AGE

Bar chart showing age from 0 to 100. Iceland: ~80, Sweden: ~77, Japan: ~77, N. Yemen: ~40, Ethiopia: ~40.

Crowded countries
(people per sq km)

Monaco	17,500
Singapore	4,475
Vatican City	2,500
Malta	1,266
Bangladesh	705
Barbados	650
Bahrain	643
Maldives	536
Mauritius	536
Taiwan	528

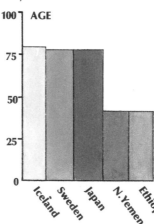

More men or women?

For every agricultural worker in Belgium there are at least 10 industrial workers. In Portugal there are almost as many people working on the land as there are in industry.

There are about 20 million more women than men living in Russia. This works out to a ratio of 7 women for every 6 men. But worldwide there are slightly more men than women.

Amazing But True

The world population in 1986 is about 5,000 million. It is increasing by 216,000 daily, which means that 150 babies are born a minute. At this rate the world's population will have doubled by 2100 AD.

The emptiest countries
(people per sq km)

Western Sahara	0.5
Mongolia	1.2
Botswana	1.8
Mauritania	1.8
Australia	2.1
Iceland	2.2
Libya	2.3
Canada	2.5
Surinam	2.5
Gabon	3.7

Where no-one is born

In the Vatican City no one is born. This is because married people do not live there. It has a population that remains around 1,000. Kenya, on the other hand, has one of the highest recorded birth rates, with a 5 per cent annual increase in population. This is over twice the worldwide average.

Religions of the world

Christianity is the largest religion, with one fifth of the world belonging to it. Islam (Muslim) is the second largest, with 600 million worshippers (just over half the number of Christians).

Amazing But True

Honduras will double its population at its present rate of increase by the year AD 2005. East Germany will take until AD 2850 to do the same.

Rich and poor countries

World incomes

Half the population of the world earns a mere 5 per cent of the world's total wealth. A very rich 15 per cent takes two thirds of this wealth.

The poorest people?

By Western standards the Tasaday tribe, who live in the Philippines, are one of the poorest people in the world. They live in caves and do not keep any animals, do not grow crops, make pots or clothes or even use wheels.

How many doctors? (people per doctor)

Top 5 countries		Bottom 5 countries	
USSR	267		
Israel	376	Ethiopia	72,582
Hungary	390	Burkina Faso	55,858
Austria	436	Malawi	47,638
United Arab		Burundi	45,430
Emirates	878	Niger	37,238

DID YOU KNOW?

In the USSR there is on average one hospital bed for every 100 people (about 2½ million beds in all). In Nigeria there is one bed for every 2,500 people (35,000 beds in the country).

How many people can read and write?
(per 1,000 people)

Top 5 countries

Australia	999	
USSR	995	
France	990	
Barbados	990	
Canada	980	

Bottom 5 countries

Niger	80	
Ethiopia	100	
Benin	110	
Afghanistan	120	
N. Yemen	130	

Electricity at home

In developed countries most homes have electricity. In poorer countries many families do not. Only 3 per cent of the homes in Haiti, 18 per cent in Paraguay and Pakistan and 25 per cent in Thailand have electricity.

Pakistan

Thailand

Paraguay

Haiti

Water in our homes

In many parts of the world only a few people are lucky enough to have piped water in their homes. In countries like Afghanistan, Ethiopia and Nepal less than one in 10 homes do.

Countries in debt

Many countries have to borrow money from world banks. These have the biggest debts:

Brazil	$102 billion*	
Mexico	$95 billion	
Argentina	$45 billion	
Venezuela	$36 billion	
Indonesia	$30 billion	

Amazing But True

The 400 richest citizens of the USA have a combined wealth of $118* billion. One saw his fortune increase by $1 billion in a year. This is 12½ million times the average annual wage of a person in Bhutan.

Privately owned cars (cars per 1,000 people)

Top 5 countries		Bottom 5 countries	
USA	499	Bangladesh	0.4
New Zealand	390	Burma	1.2
Canada	389	India	1.2
Australia	368	Burundi	1.3
Luxembourg	365	Chad	1.5

Rich and poor countries

(To find out the average annual income for people in different countries, we have taken the wealth a country makes in a year and divided it evenly between the people who live there.)

Qatar	£22,350*
United Arab Emirates	£20,000
Switzerland	£14,000
USA	£10,000
Malawi	£170
Burma	£150
Bhutan	£130
Bangladesh	£110

*See page 96

Natural products

Top 5 wool producers
(tonnes per year)

Australia	722,000
USSR	460,000
New Zealand	363,000
China	205,000
Argentina	155,000

Most important fibre

Cotton is the world's most important fibre. It was made into cloth over 3,000 years ago in India and Central America. Today it is used to make lace, clothes, sheets, carpets, and industrial products such as thread, film, plastics and special paper.

Amazing But True

The Dutch grow and sell about 3,000 million flowers a year. This is 80,000 flowers for every sq km in the country.

Most expensive oil

The most expensive oil used in perfumes is Musk oil. It sells at $633* for 28 gms or 1 oz. It comes from glands of the male Musk deer, which are found in the mountains of Korea and Mongolia.

Fastest growing plant

Bamboo, used for making window blinds, furniture, floor mats and poles, is one of the fastest growing plants. It can shoot up 90 cms (36 ins) in a day and reaches a height of around 30 m (100 ft). It grows in India, the Far East and China.

Top 5 cotton producers
(tonnes per year)

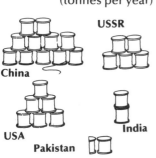

China	5,700,000
USA	2,913,000
USSR	2,400,000
India	1,250,000
Pakistan	860,000

Top 5 tobacco producers
(tonnes per year)

China	1,523,000
USA	640,000
India	594,000
Brazil	400,000
USSR	350,000

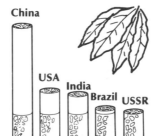

*See page 96

Expensive spice

One of the most expensive spices is saffron. It comes from a crocus flower and is used to colour and give an aroma to rice dishes. Grown in China, France, Spain and Iran, over 200,000 stamens are needed to make ½ kilo (1 lb).

The secret of silk

Silk comes from the cocoon of the silkworm. One cocoon contains about a kilometre of thread. It came originally from China, where for hundreds of years its source was kept a secret. One story tells us that in 140 BC a Chinese princess hid some eggs of the silkworm in her hair and took them to Turkestan. From there silk was brought to Europe.

Top 5 rubber producers

	(tonnes per year)
Malaysia	1,625,000
Indonesia	1,100,000
Thailand	650,000
India	185,000
Sri Lanka	140,000

Amazing But True

Wild ginseng roots, found in China and Korea, sell for £10,000*for 28 gms (1 oz).

DID YOU KNOW?

Tobacco was first smoked by the American Indians. It was brought to Europe in the 16th century as an ornamental plant. The habit of smoking the dried leaves did not catch on until some years later.

Where rubber comes from

Rubber comes from the sap (called latex) of the rubber tree. To drain it out, the bark has to be cut. Long before Europeans explored the jungles of Central and South America (the original home of the rubber tree) Indians were using latex to waterproof their clothes and footwear.

Best quality wool

Merino wool comes from a breed of sheep that was originally found in Spain. It is considered the best quality wool.

*See page 96

Fuel and energy

Top 10 coal producers
(millions of tonnes per year)

China	763	India	136
USA	751	Australia	125
USSR	485	W. Germany	85
Poland	192	Britain	51
South Africa	140	Czechoslovakia	27

World's largest oil platform

The largest oil platform is the Statfjord B, built at Stavanger in Norway. It weighs 816,000 tonnes, cost £1.1 billion*to construct and needed 8 tugs to tow it into position. It is the heaviest object ever moved in one piece.

DID YOU KNOW?

More than one third of the world's population still depends on wood for fuel. In some areas of Africa and Asia, timber provides 80 per cent of energy needs. This is equivalent to the use developed nations make of gas and nuclear power.

Fuel consumption

An average American uses about 1,000 times as much fuel in his or her life as does an average Nepalese citizen and about twice as much as a European.

Top 10 importers of oil
(millions of tonnes per year)

Japan	183
USA	170
France	70
W. Germany	67
Italy	66
Netherlands	44
Spain	41
Britain	32
Brazil	24
Belgium	18

Nuclear submarines

The first nuclear-powered submarine (The Nautilus) was built in the USA in 1955. It travelled 530,000 km (330,000 miles) using only 5 kg (12 lb) of nuclear fuel. A car covering the same distance at an average speed would use 38,000 litres of petrol (8,250 gallons).

Amazing But True

If we could make use of all solar, wind, water and wave power that exists on the earth's surface, we would have 20 billion times as much energy as we need at present.

*See page 96

Longest oil pipeline

The longest oil pipeline stretches from Edmonton, Canada, to Buffalo in New York State, USA. This is a distance of 2,856 km (1,775 miles). If it were laid out like a road, it would take a car 2 days to drive along it doing an average speed of 60 km (38 miles) an hour.

Fuels used in industry since 1850

	1850	1900	1950	2000
Wood	65%	37%	—	—
Coal	10%	55%	59%	—
Oil	—	8%	32%	15%
Gas	—	—	9%	48%
Nuclear	—	—	—	37%

Cause for alarm

By the year AD 2100 some scientists believe that the world could have run out of oil, coal and gas. This may cause some problems as it has also been estimated that we will be using 5½ times as much energy as today.

DID YOU KNOW?

Waterwheels were used in Rome over 2,000 years ago to grind corn. Water power is still used in parts of the world.

Top exporters of oil

(millions of tonnes per year)

Saudi Arabia	168
USSR	129
Britain	79
Iran	78
Mexico	78
United Arab Emirates	60
Nigeria	52
Venezuela	52
Libya	45
Indonesia	41
Iraq	41

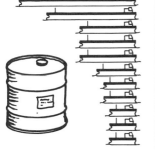

Top 5 producers of uranium (nuclear fuel)

(tonnes per year)

Canada	9,200
USA	7,200
South Africa	5,700
Australia	4,390
Namibia	3,700

Amazing But True

One tonne of nuclear fuel (uranium) can produce as much energy as 20,000 tonnes of coal. The first nuclear power station was opened in the USSR in 1954.

Metals and precious gems

World's deepest mine

The Western Deep gold mine in South Africa is 3,480 m (12,720 ft) deep. This makes it almost 9 times deeper than the tallest building is high and about 2½ times deeper than the deepest cave. It has a temperature up to 55°C (131°F) at the bottom and is cooled by special refrigerators for people working there.

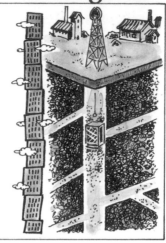

Top 5 copper producer
(tonnes per year)

Chile	1,290,000
USA	1,091,000
USSR	1,020,000
Canada	712,000
Zambia	565,000

Lighter than steel

Aluminium is used to make beer and soft drink cans. A very light metal, it is replacing steel in such things as aircraft, cars, cameras, window-frames and bicycles.

Top 5 tin producers
(tonnes per year)

Malaysia	41,000
Indonesia	23,000
Thailand	21,000
Brazil	20,000
USSR	17,000

Commonest precious metal

Silver is the commonest precious metal. It is lighter than gold. About half the silver mined is used as a coating for photographic film.

Largest underground mine

The San Manuel Mine in Arizona, USA, is the largest underground mine. This copper mine has over 573 km (350 miles) of tunnels. If laid out in a straight line, the tunnels would reach Los Angeles, California.

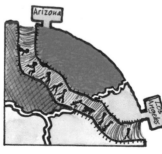

Amazing But True

South Africa produces 3 times as much gold each year as its nearest rival, the USSR. It mines 595 million gms (21 million ozs): 28 gms or 1 oz of pure gold can be beaten into a fine wire that would stretch 88 km (55 miles).

Top 10 iron ore miners
(tonnes per year)

USSR	135,000,000
Brazil	61,000,000
China	61,000,000
Australia	57,000,000
USA	35,000,000
India	26,000,000
Canada	25,000,000
South Africa	15,000,000
Liberia	11,000,000
Sweden	11,000,000

Worth its weight

Platinum is the most expensive metal in the world. Unlike silver, it does not tarnish and is used in jewellery for mounting precious gems.

Top 5 lead producers
(tonnes per year)

USA	920,000
USSR	800,000
Japan	362,000
W. Germany	357,000
Britain	338,000

Top 5 aluminium miners
(tonnes per year)

Australia	32,000,000
Guinea	14,700,000
Jamaica	8,700,000
Brazil	6,300,000
USSR	6,200,000

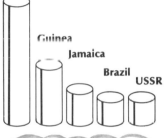

The oldest gems

India has records going back to 300 BC that tell us about the mining of moonstones, sapphires, diamonds, emeralds, garnets and agates.

The golden fleece

Some streams and rivers carry gold particles after running over rocks containing the precious metal. An ancient method of extracting this gold was to put a sheep's fleece in the stream, trapping the tiny pieces of metal in the wool.

A tough gem

Diamonds are 90 times harder than any other naturally occuring substance. Some are used in industry for cutting very hard substances. Dentists use them on their drills.

City of Jewels

Ratnapura, in Sri Lanka, is known as the 'City of Jewels' because of the amazing variety of gems found there. These include sapphires, diamonds and rubies.

*See page 96

Business and industry

Top 5 car producers

(cars per year)

USA	7,700,000
Japan	7,073,000
W. Germany	3,788,000
France	2,910,000
USSR	1,300,000

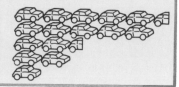

DID YOU KNOW?

China makes three times as many bicycles as its closest rivals, the USA and Japan. If the 17½ million made in a year were ridden end to end they would stretch three quarters of the way round the world.

Giant companies

Exxon, a giant oil company in New York, earns more money in a year than many countries. Its sales have reached as high as $90,000 million*, which is about equal to the national income of Belgium.

Stock exchanges

Stock Exchanges are places where governments and companies sell shares and raise money. There are 138 in the world at present, the oldest being in Amsterdam which dates from 1602. The London Stock Exchange alone does over £1,000 million* worth of business a day.

Most expensive land

Land in the centre of Hong Kong costs £120,000 per sq m (£11,000 per sq ft) to rent. Even a small company could expect to pay up to £1 million* per year for floor space.

The largest tanker

The *Seawise Giant,* a Japanese supertanker built in 1981, is the largest tanker in the world. It is almost ½ km (a third of a mile) long, equal to about 5 football pitches end to end. It can carry 565,000 tonnes of crude oil around the world. It would take 15 of these supertankers to supply the USA with her daily needs of imported oil, or 5,500 tankers every year.

Who makes the most?

(amount produced per year)

Typewriters	Japan	2,998,000
Refrigerators	USSR	5,933,000
Socks	USSR	976,000,000
Calculators	Japan	52,435,000
Pianos	Japan	360,338

*See page 96

The power of oil

Over 30 countries in the world make money from exporting only one thing – oil. The biggest producers are Saudi Arabia, USSR, United Arab Emirates and Nigeria. Saudi Arabia alone has one third of world output. Oil accounts for one quarter of world trade.

Top 5 radio producers
(radios per year)

Hong Kong	47,986,000
China	19,990,000
Singapore	15,165,000
Japan	13,338,000
USA	11,089,000

Top 5 TV producers
(sets per year)

Japan	13,275,000
USA	12,084,000
USSR	8,578,000
South Korea	7,641,000
China	6,840,000

Largest papermill

The Union Camp Corporation at Savannah, USA, is the largest paper mill, producing almost 100,000 tonnes of paper a year. This is equal to about 28,000,000 sheets of A4 paper, or 250,000 paperback books, a day.

The oldest company

The Faversham Oyster Fishery Company, Britain, has been going since before 1189. This makes it the oldest company on record.

Advertising products

The USA spends more money on advertising than all the other countries of the world put together. In 1978,

Amazing But True

Nippon Steel of Tokyo, Japan, produces about 27 million tonnes of steel a year. This is enough to cover all of Spain and Portugal if the steel was beaten out paper-thin.

during the Super Bowl football match final, the price of advertising on American TV was $325,000* a minute.

Farming

Top grain and bean producers
(tonnes per year)

Soya beans	USA	43,969,000
Barley	USSR	54,500,000
Corn (maize)	USA	106,300,000
Wheat	USSR	82,000,000
Rice	China	172,000,000

Top 5 potato growers
(tonnes per year)

USSR	83,000,000
China	50,000,000
Poland	34,551,000
USA	14,742,000
India	10,100,000

Top 5 banana growers
(tonnes per year)

Brazil	6,692,000	
Ecuador	2,000,000	
Mexico	1,624,000	
Colombia	1,280,000	
Honduras	1,250,000	

A field of wheat

About 750 years ago, an average sized field of wheat may have provided enough food for 5 people for a year. Today, the same field in a developed country would feed between 20 and 50 people for a year and supply enough seed to sow for the next crop.

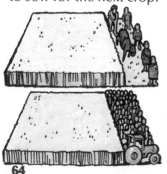

DID YOU KNOW?

The amount of protein produced from a field of soya beans is 13 times greater than the same field used to graze cattle for meat.

Largest mixed farms

The world's largest mixed (arable and dairy) farms are in the USSR. Farms of over 25,000 hectares (62,000 acres) are not uncommon. This is over 600 times larger than the world's smallest country, the Vatican City, and twice the size of Malta.

Top 5 beef producers
(tonnes per year)

USA	10,951,000
USSR	7,200,000
Argentina	2,510,000
EEC	2,506,000
Brazil	2,200,000

Top 5 milk producers
(tonnes per year)

USSR	89,600,000
USA	61,553,000
France	34,500,000
W. Germany	25,550,000
UK	16,720,000

A land of sheep

In Australia there are more than 3 times as many sheep as people. The largest sheep station is in South Australia. It is 1,040,000 hectares (2,560,000 acres). This is larger than Cyprus.

Top 5 grape growers
(tonnes per year)

Italy	12,255,000
France	8,550,000
USSR	7,200,000
Spain	5,046,000
USA	4,796,000

Top 5 sugar producers
(tonnes per year)

Brazil	9,200,000
USSR	8,150,000
Cuba	7,800,000
India	6,420,000
China	5,040,000

Experiments with food

What do you get when you cross the American buffalo with an ordinary cow? The beefalo of course! This animal has been bred to produce more meat to help world food production.

DID YOU KNOW?

American scientists have predicted that they will be able to breed cows weighing 4.5 tonnes. This is about the size of an elephant.

Amazing But True

A certain type of bacteria grown on petrol can be used as a source of food. The bacteria multiplies at a rate of 32,000,000 a day. It is harvested and processed into a highly nutritious food.

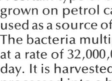

Bacteria Pizza with chips

BACTERIA SAUCE

Bacteria Burger

Chef's special Triple decker Bacteria Sandwich

Top 5 butter producers
(tonnes per year)

USSR	1,290,000
India	730,000
France	600,000
USA	595,000
W. Germany	530,000

Forestry

Top 5 softwood producers
(cubic metres per year)

USSR	86,000,000
USA	54,000,000
Canada	38,000,000
Japan	30,000,000
Sweden	10,000,000

Top 5 hardwood producers
(cubic metres per year)

USA	17,000,000
USSR	12,000,000
China	8,000,000
Japan	7,000,000
Malaysia	5,000,000

The tallest tree

The largest living thing on earth is the giant redwood tree, growing in the USA and Canada. The tallest is 112 m (367 ft) high. This is considerably taller than the Statue of Liberty, New York, which stands at 93 m (305 ft).

DID YOU KNOW?

The fastest growing tree in the world is the Eucalyptus. One tree in New Guinea grew 10.5 m (35 ft) in 1 year. This is almost 3 cm (over 1 in) a day. In contrast, a Sika Spruce inside the Arctic Circle takes some 98 years to grow 28 cm (11 in); some 4,000 times slower.

Forests in peril

Nearly half the world's rain forests have been cut down and are still being cut down at a rate of 24 sq km (9 sq miles) an hour or 200,000 sq km (80,000 sq miles) a year – an area almost the size of Britain.

The rubber tree

Rubber trees were originally found only in the Amazon rain forest. In 1876 Sir Henry Wickham shipped 70,000 seeds to Kew Gardens in London. Seedlings were then sent to Sri Lanka and Malaysia where rubber plantations were started.

The oldest tree

Some bristlecone pines found in California, USA, are over 4,500 years old.

The lightest wood

Wood from the Balsa tree weighs 40 kg per cubic metre (2½ lb per cubic ft). It is the world's lightest wood. The black ironwood tree is forty times heavier.

World's largest forest

About 25 per cent of the world's forests cover an area of the northern USSR and Scandinavia up to the Arctic Circle. It is the world's largest forest.

World of trees

There are about 40 million sq km (25,000,000 sq miles) of forest in the world. This is about equal to the area of the 3 largest countries (USSR, Canada and China).

Top 5 producers of paper
(tonnes per year)

USA	54,117,000
Japan	15,880,000
W. Germany	7,619,000
China	5,745,000
France	5,041,000

A tree of gold

In 1959 a nursery in the USA bought a single Golden Delicious apple tree for $51,000 (at the time, £18,214)*, making it the most expensive tree the world has known.

Amazing But True

A fire raged non-stop for 10 months from September 1982 in Borneo. It spread over 36,000 sq km (22,000 sq miles). In all, about 13,500 sq km (8,000 sq miles) of forest was destroyed. Several rare species of trees and wild life were made extinct.

*See page 96

Fishing

Freezer trawlers

Fish caught at sea are often frozen on board the trawlers. They are gutted and left in piles to freeze together. Once back in port, they are defrosted, filleted and sold.

Top fish-eating nation

The Japanese eat their way through 3,400 million kg (7,500 million lbs) of fish a year. This means that each person has an average 30 kg (65 lbs) of fish a year. They are the world's biggest fish-eating nation. Their nearest rivals, the Scandinavians, eat only half as much fish on average and the Americans only one fifth.

The most expensive fish

The Russian sturgeon fetches the highest price of any fish in the world. The eggs of the female sturgeon (caviare) are a prized delicacy. The best caviare costs over £28 for 50 gms (1¾ ozs) or £570 per kg. (£258 per lb).*

Amazing But True

Over 95 per cent of all the fish caught in the world are caught in the Northern Hemisphere.

DID YOU KNOW?

A special substance found in the scales of some fish (especially herrings) is used to make a paint. This paint is coated on to glass beads to make imitation pearls.

Top 5 most caught fish
(millions of tonnes per year)

Alaska Pollack	4.5
Japanese Pilchard	4
Chilean Pilchard	3.25
Atlantic Cod	2.25
Chilean Jack Mackerel	2

Top 3 oyster catchers
(tonnes per year)

Japan	250,288
Korea	189,204
USA	81,336

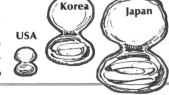

*See page 96

Greatest catch

The most fish ever caught in one haul was made by a Norwegian trawler. It is estimated that in one net it pulled on board more than 120 million fish; over 2,400 tonnes in all. This is enough to feed every man, woman and child in Norway for two weeks.

Largest fishing vessel

A whaling factory ship built in the USSR in 1971, called *The Vostok* weighs 26,400 tonnes making it the largest fishing vessel in the world. It is 224.5 m (736.7 ft) long, which means that you could fit 9½ tennis courts end to end along its deck.

Fishing with birds

In Japan, cormorants are trained to catch fish and to fly back to a boat. Each bird is stopped from swallowing the fish by a tight leather collar round its neck.

Fish farming

Many countries now breed fish in special underwater farms. These are the leading countries in this sort of farming:

(in tonnes per year)

China	2,300,000
India	600,000
USSR	300,000
Japan	250,000
Indonesia	240,000

DID YOU KNOW?

Out of all the fish caught in the world, about three quarters are eaten as food. The other quarter is used to make such things as glue, soap, margarine, pet food and fertilizer.

Amazing But True

A prehistoric fish that was thought to have become extinct about 70 million years ago, was caught in the sea off South Africa. It is called the coelacanth and since 1938 many more of these fish have been caught.

Top 5 fishing countries
(tonnes per year)

Japan	11,800,000	
USSR	10,500,000	
China	6,193,000	
USA	4,741,000	
Chile	4,499,000	

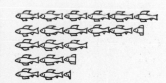

Food and drink

How many calories?

Calories measure the energy content of different foods. We all need a certain amount every day to make our bodies work properly. People in Europe and the USA eat about 3,500 calories a day. Many people in Asia and Africa get at most 2,700. Some people in these countries live on a very poor diet. This may consist of beans, vegetables and grains, and be too low in calories and protein.

Top 5 wine producers
(hectolitres per year)

Italy	75,000,000
France	69,000,000
Spain	42,430,000
USSR	32,248,000
Argentina	23,302,000

Top 5 beer producers
(hectolitres per year)

USA	229,000,000
W. Germany	91,000,000
USSR	66,000,000
Britain	60,000,000
Japan	50,000,000

A world-wide drink

There are 171 countries in the world and Coca-cola is sold in about 157 of them. In one day, sales reached about 280 million cans. This means that if all the cans sold in one month were placed on top of each other they would make three chains each reaching the moon.

DID YOU KNOW?

The largest cake ever was baked in New Jersey, USA, in 1982. It weighed in at 37 tonnes – equal to the weight of 7 elephants.

Meals within meals

Bedouin sometimes prepare a meal of stuffed, roast camel for wedding feasts. They start by stuffing a fish with eggs, putting this inside a chicken, the chicken inside a whole roast sheep and the lot inside a cooked camel.

Most nutritious fruit

The avocado pear contains about 165 calories for every 100 gms of edible fruit. This is more than eggs or milk. It also contains twice as much protein as milk, and more vitamin A, B and C. In contrast, the cucumber has only 16 calories per 100 gms.

Most expensive food

The First Choice Black Perigord truffle, found in France, costs £8.50 for a 12.5 g (½ oz tin) or £680 a kg (£309 per pound).*

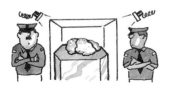

Top 5 honey producers
(tonnes per year)

USSR	193,000
China	115,000
USA	81,600
Mexico	62,000
Argentina	34,000

Top 5 tea growers
(tonnes per year)

India	565,000
China	397,000
Sri Lanka	190,000
USSR	140,000
Japan	99,000

Top 5 coffee producers
(tonnes per year)

Brazil	1,003,000
Colombia	840,000
Indonesia	266,000
Ivory Coast	250,000
Mexico	234,000

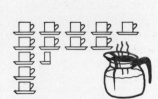

Super sausage

A sausage-maker in Birmingham, Britain, made one specimen that was 9 km (5½ miles) long. This amounts to about 87,000 ordinary sausages.

*See page 96

A monster melon

The largest melon weighed over 90 kg (14 stone). The size of a large human being, it would have fed 400 people.

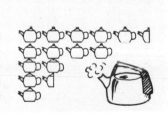

Buildings and structures

The largest hotel

It would take more than 8½ years for one person to sleep in every room of the Hotel Rossiya, Moscow. The 3,200 rooms can put up 5,350 guests. There are 93 lifts and about 3,000 staff.

DID YOU KNOW?

The most expensive hotel in the world is the Hotel Nova Park in Elysées in Paris, France. The Royale Suite costs £3,525*a night. This is more than many French people earn in a year.

World's longest wall

The Great Wall of China stretches for 3,460 km (2,150 miles), ranges between 4½ and 12 m (15 and 40 ft) high, and is up to 10 m (32 ft) thick. Another 2,860 km (1,780 miles) can be added because of spurs and kinks. This makes it as long as the River Nile, the longest river in the world. Six Great Walls laid end to end would reach round the circumference of the Earth.

The largest palace

The Imperial Palace in the centre of Beijing, China, covers an area of 72 hectares (178 acres). This is equal to 100 football pitches. It is surrounded by the largest moat in the world – 38 km (23½ miles) in length.

The tallest buildings

Sears Tower, Chicago, USA	443 metres
World Trade Center, New York, USA	411 metres
Empire State Building, New York, USA	381 metres
Standard Oil Building, Chicago, USA	346 metres
John Hancock Center, Chicago, USA	343 metres
Chrysler Building, New York, USA	319 metres
Bank of China, Hong Kong	315 metres
60 Wall Tower, New York, USA	290 metres
First Canadian Place, Toronto, Canada	289 metres
40 Wall Tower, New York, USA	282 metres

Highest homes

The highest settlement is on the Indian and Tibetan border. Basisi is 5,988 m (19,650 ft) above sea level. This is only 2,860 m (9,384 ft) lower than Mount Everest, the highest mountain in the world.

*See page 96

The highest dam

The highest dam is in Switzerland. The Grande Dixence is 285 m (935 ft) from the base to the rim and cost a staggering £151 million* in 1961 when it was completed. This is only 15 m (50 ft) short of the Eiffel Tower in Paris.

The tallest lighthouse

The steel tower lighthouse in Yokohama, Japan, is 106 m (348 ft) high. But almost 7 of these would be needed standing on top of each other to reach the world's tallest structure, the Warszawa Radio Mast in Poland.

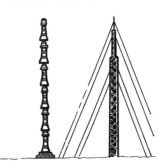

The oldest buildings

Twenty-one huts were discovered in 1960 in Nice, France, that have been dated to 400,000 BC. They are the oldest recognizable buildings in the world.

Smallest house

A fisherman's cottage in North Wales has only 2 tiny rooms and a staircase inside. The outside measures 1.8 m (6 ft) wide and only just over 3 m (10 ft) high.

Seven Wonders

The Seven Wonders of the World were first mentioned in the 2nd century BC by a man called Antipater of Sidon. They were:

The Pyramids of Giza, Egypt
The Hanging Gardens of Babylon, Iraq
The Tomb of King Mausolus, Turkey
The Temple of Diana, Ephesus, Turkey
The Colossus of Rhodes, Greece
The Statue of Jupiter, Olympia, Greece
The Pharos of Alexandria, Egypt

Of the Seven Wonders, only the pyramids are still standing. The others have been destroyed by fire, earthquake and invading nations.

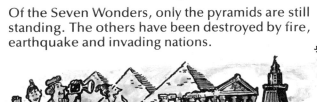

Cities

Fastest growing city

Mexico City is at present growing at a rate of 25 per cent every 5 years. With a population of 16 million it is estimated that by the year 2000, it will be over 31 million. This is 5 times as many people as there are in all Switzerland at present.

The largest town

Mount Isa, Queensland, Australia, spreads over almost 41,000 sq km (15,800 sq miles). It covers an area 26 times greater than that of London and is about the same size as Switzerland.

Top 10 most crowded cities
(people per city)

Mexico City	16,000,000
Sao Paulo	12,600,000
Shanghai	11,900,000
Tokyo	11,600,000
Buenos Aires	9,700,000
Beijing	9,200,000
Calcutta	9,200,000
New York	9,100,000
Rio de Janeiro	9,000,000
Paris	8,500,000

Traffic City

The greatest amount of vehicles in any city is to be found in Los Angeles, USA. At one interchange almost 500,000 vehicles were counted in a 24-hour period during a weekday. This is an average of 20,000 cars and trucks an hour.

The cheapest city

In 1626 a Dutchman bought an island in America from some local Indians. He gave them some cloth and beads worth about $24 for an area of land he thought covered 86 sq km (34 sq miles). In fact it was 57 sq km (22 sq miles). But it was still a bargain. He had bought Manhattan, now one of the most crowded and expensive islands in the world. He named his town New Amsterdam but it was later renamed New York.

How many people live in cities?

About one third of people in the world live in towns or cities. By the year 2000, experts believe that over half will live in urban areas. But this may vary from place to place. In the USA about 74 per cent live in towns and cities compared with 20 per cent in India.

The oldest city

Archaeologists believe that Jericho, in Jordan, is the oldest continuously inhabited place. There were as many as 3,000 people living there as early as 7,800 BC.

Longest underground

London has 400 km (247 miles) of underground tracks, making it the longest in the world. This includes 267 stations and about 450 trains. All the track laid end to end would stretch from London to Land's End in Cornwall.

An island city

Venice, in the north of Italy, is built on 118 islands in a lagoon. Canals serve as streets and roads and everybody uses boats instead of cars to get around. There are over 400 bridges crossing the canals.

Poles apart

The most northerly capital is Reykjavik in Iceland. The southernmost is Wellington, New Zealand. They are 20,000 km (12,500 miles) apart.

So far from the sea

Urungi, capital of the Uighur Autonomous Region in China, is the furthest city from the sea. It is about 2,250 km (1,400 miles) from the nearest coast.

The longest name

Krung Thep is the shortened name of the capital of Thailand, known in the West as Bangkok. Its full name has 167 letters and means in English,

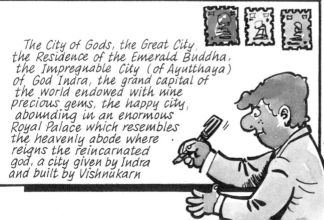

The City of Gods, the Great City, the Residence of the Emerald Buddha, the Impregnable City (of Ayutthaya) of God Indra, the grand capital of the world endowed with nine precious gems, the happy city, abounding in an enormous Royal Palace which resembles the heavenly abode where reigns the reincarnated god, a city given by Indra and built by Vishnukarn

Communications

Telephones – top 5 countries
(per 1,000 people)

Country	per 1,000
Monaco	1,071
Sweden	828
USA	788
Switzerland	741
Canada	670

Televisions – top 5 countries
(per 1,000 people)

Country	per 1,000
Monaco	654
USA	624
Japan	537
Canada	476
Italy	390

Largest and smallest book

The smallest published book measures 1.4 x 1.4 mm. Only 200 copies were printed in Tokyo, Japan. The book is a children's story called *Ari (The Ant)*. Over 4 million copies would fit on the cover of the world's largest book (the *Super Book*), which measures 2.74 x 3.07 m (9 x 10 ft).

Secret codes

Coded messages have been used since 400 BC. Probably the best known is the Morse code, invented in the 19th century by Samuel Morse.

Newspapers – top 10 countries
(bought daily per 1,000 people)

Country	per 1,000
Japan	575
Liechtenstein	558
E. Germany	530
Sweden	524
Finland	515
Norway	483
Britain	421
Iceland	420
Monaco	410
W. Germany	408

Dates of famous inventions

Telephone	1876
Gramophone	1877
Moving film	1885
Television	1934
Audio film	1927
Tape recorder	1935
Photocopier	1938
Computer	1946
Transistor radio	1948
Stereo recording	1958
Microcomputer	1969

Amazing But True

A black and white TV with a 3.5 cm (1⅖ in) screen was designed and made by Seiko in Japan. It fits on to a wrist watch. The smallest colour TV has a 21 cm (8 in) screen.

Longest telephone cable

A telephone cable running beneath the Pacific Ocean links Canada and Australia via New Zealand and the Hawaiian Islands. It is 14,500 km (9,000 miles) long and cost £35 million* in 1963 to build.

Crossed wires

The Pentagon, Washington DC, is the centre of American defence. It has the largest switchboard in the world. About 25,000 telephone lines can be used at the same time.

*See page 96

Mail bag

The USA has the largest postal service in the world. In one year its citizens sent over 120 billion letters and packages. This is equal to 521 letters a year or about 1½ letters a day, for everyone living in America.

Communicating flags

Semaphore is a method of signalling with flags. With one flag in each hand, the signaller holds them in different positions to spell out the alphabet. A way of passing messages over a short distance, it was invented by the French army in 1792 during the French Revolution.

Computers for the disabled

The *Sprite* is a piece of computer technology that has been designed to imitate the human voice. It helps those with speech problems.

A long-distance chat

Men have talked to each other directly between the moon and the earth, a distance of 400,000 km (250,000 miles), making this the longest distance chat. A powerful radio signal sent into space is expected to take 24,000 years to reach its destination, a group of stars 10 billion times further away than the moon. It could be the longest awaited reply.

A golden pen

The ballpoint pen was invented in 1938 by a Hungarian named Biro. In its first year in the UK 53 million were sold.

Newspaper facts

When *The Times* newspaper reported Nelson's victory over the French at the Battle of Trafalgar in 1805, the news took 2½ weeks to reach London. When the same newspaper, 164 years later, showed pictures of the first men on the moon, they came out only a few hours after the landing.

DID YOU KNOW?

The world's first postage stamp was the *Penny Black,* issued in Britain in May, 1840. A one-cent British Guiana stamp of 1856, of which there is only one known example, is thought to be worth £500,000.*

Shrinking world

Using satellites orbiting the earth, television can now reach a potential audience of about 2½ billion people. An event like the Olympic Games, can be beamed live into the homes of half the people in the world.

Travel

Airship travel

Hydrogen-filled airships were in regular use up until 1938, taking people across the Atlantic. They were stopped because too many caught on fire.

Road building

To move their armies the Romans built over 80,000 km (50,000 miles) of road in Europe and the Middle East. After their conquest of Britain, it took only 6 days by horse to get from London to Rome. About 1,500 years later in the 19th century, it took just as long.

Most travelled person

An American, named Jesse Rosdall, went to all the countries and territories in the world except North Korea and the French Antarctic. He claimed to have travelled a total of 2,617,766 km (1,626,605 miles). This is equal to almost 7 trips to the moon or 65 journeys round the world.

Petrol consumption

In the USA over 1,400 million litres (300 million gallons) of petrol a day are used. This is enough petrol in a year to fill an oil drum 36.5 km (22.6 miles) high and 26.5 km (16.5 miles) wide. A total of over 20,000 km^3, it would fill Lake Baykal in the USSR, the lake with the greatest volume.

Top 5 road countries
(kilometres of road)

USA	6,365,590
Canada	3,002,000
France	1,502,000
Brazil	1,411,936
USSR	1,408,800

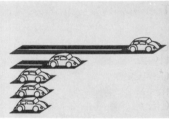

Longest and shortest flight

The shortest scheduled flight (from the island of Westray to Papa Westray off Scotland, lasting 2 minutes) could be made over 450 times while one jet makes a non-stop journey from Sydney to San Francisco, a total of 7,475 km (4,645 miles).

The first car

The first petrol-driven car took to the roads in 1885. It had 3 wheels and a tiller to steer. Its top speed was 16 kph (10 mph). Just 100 years later there are enough vehicles in the world for every tenth person to own one. If they all met in one traffic jam, it would go round the world 34 times.

DID YOU KNOW?

Concorde travels faster than the speed of sound, cruising at 2,333 kph (1,500 mph). It flies between London and New York in 3 hours, a distance of 5,536 km (3,500 miles). This is over twice as fast as an ordinary passenger plane.

Widest and narrowest

The widest road in the world is the Monumental Axis in Brasilia, Brazil. It is 250 m (820 ft) wide, which is wide enough for 160 cars side by side. It is over 500 times wider than the narrowest street, which is in Port Isaac, Britain. At its narrowest it is a mere 49 cm (1½ ft) and is known as 'squeeze-belly alley'.

World famous train

The Orient Express once ran between Paris and Istanbul. It now makes a shorter trip from London to Venice. It offers the highest luxury in travel. A one-way ticket costs at present £475.* This is also the price of a single airfare to Sydney, Australia, a city 14 times further away from London than Venice.

Busiest rail network

About 18½ million people use trains in Japan every day. If one train carried them all, it would have about 370,000 carriages and would stretch for over 3,300 km (2,000 miles).

Fastest train

A special passenger train (called a TGV) which runs between Paris and Lyons, France, has an average speed of 212.5 kph (132 mph). It reaches 270 kph (168 mph) on its 425 km (264 mile) journey, which takes 2 hours in all.

Top 5 railway countries
(kilometres of track)

USA	288,072
USSR	240,400
Canada	67,066
India	60,933
China	50,000

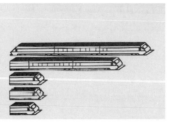

Amazing But True

The Boeing 747 (Jumbo Jet) is the largest and most powerful plane. It can carry up to 500 passengers. It stands as high as a 6-storey office block and weighs over 370 tonnes. It has a maximum speed of 969 kph (602 mph) and a wing-span of over 70 m (232 ft).

The bicycle

An early form of bicycle, called a hobbyhorse or walk-along, was popular in the mid-17th century. It had no pedals. We had to wait almost 200 years for their invention.

Top holiday countries
(number of visitors)

Italy	48,311,474
Spain	42,011,000
France	33,156,000
USA	23,086,000
Austria	14,253,000
Canada	12,183,000
UK	11,637,000
W. Germany	9,460,000
Switzerland	9,186,000
Hungary	6,473,000

*See page 96

Money*

World's largest mint

The largest mint – the factory where coins are made – is in the USA. It can make 22 million coins a day using almost 100 stamping machines. It covers an area of 4½ hectares (11 acres). At full production it could produce a pile of coins 5 times higher than Mount Everest in just one day.

Earliest coins

Coins found in Lydia (Turkey) date from the reign of King Gyges in the 7th century BC. These coins below were found in Sicily and date to the 5th century BC.

Highest value note

A few, very rare, $10,000* notes exist in America. They are not in general circulation.

Amazing But True

The American ambassador to India handed over in 1974 a cheque for 16,640 million rupees (£852,791,660)*on behalf of his government to the Indian government. It was the largest cheque ever written.

Military spending

The USA spends over $500 billion*on defence in a year which is more than all the people in China, India and Indonesia earn in the same period. The USA and the USSR together spend more on arms than the rest of the world.

Highest paid job

The chairman of the First Boston Corporation, an American-based company, earned $5,215 a day in 1984. This made an annual salary of $2 million (£1,200,000).*

Sunken treasure

Almost 2,000 Spanish galleons lie off the coast of Florida and the Bahamas. They were sunk in the 16th century, most of them carrying large amounts of gold. This area is the largest untapped storehouse of treasure in the world.

Golden Beatle

Paul McCartney, songwriter and ex-Beatle, earns an estimated £25 million a year from his records. This is about £45 a minute or £70,000*a day.

The Chinese one kwan note printed in the 14th century was 92.8 x 33 cm (9 x 13 in). It is 73 times larger than the smallest note, the 10 bani issued in Romania in 1917.

Income Tax

Many governments take a certain amount of money from the salaries of their citizens. This is called Income Tax. It was introduced in Britain in 1799 by the Prime Minister, William Pitt. He needed money to pay for the war against Napoleon. The war ended over 150 years ago, but Income Tax has remained.

Different money

Coins and notes are not the only form of money. Teeth of animals, metal bracelets and necklaces, shells, axe heads, knives, blocks of salt and even blocks of tea leaves have been used. The word *cash* comes from an Indian word meaning compressed tea and the word *salary* comes from the Latin word for salt. Both were used to pay people in the past.

Honesty rules

In 1972 $500,000[*] was found by a man in Lower Elliot, USA. The money was dropped by a criminal escaping by parachute. Resisting the temptation to keep the money, he tracked down the owner and returned every cent.

Powerful banks

The world's most wealthy bank is Citicorp, based in New York. Only the US Government handles more money in a year. The 56 poorest countries each has less wealth than each of the top 500 commercial banks in the world.

Money loses value

When the price of buying things goes up, money becomes worth less. This is called inflation. In Germany after the First World War, the German Mark dropped in value. In 1921, 81 Marks were worth 1 American dollar. Two years later, the same dollar was worth 1 million Marks.

Great Train Robbery

In 1963 over £2½ million[*] was stolen from a train in Buckinghamshire, England. Only one seventh of the total was ever recovered. It was the costliest train robbery.

Languages

10 most spoken languages

Chinese	700,000,000
English	400,000,000
Russian	265,000,000
Spanish	240,000,000
Hindustani	230,000,000
Arabic	146,000,000
Portuguese	145,000,000
Bengali	144,000,000
German	119,000,000
Japanese	116,000,000

The first alphabet

The Phoenicians, who once lived where Syria, Jordan and Lebanon are today, had an alphabet of 29 letters as early as 1,700 BC. It was adopted by the Greeks and the Romans. Through the Romans, who went on to conquer most of Europe, it became the alphabet of Western countries.

Sounds strange

One tribe of Mexican Indians hold entire conversations just by whistling. The different pitches provide meaning.

The Rosetta Stone

The Rosetta Stone was found by Napoleon in the sands of Egypt. It dates to about 196 BC. On it is an inscription in hieroglyphics and a translation in Greek. Because scholars knew ancient Greek, they could work out what the Egyptian hieroglyphics meant. From this they learned the language of the ancient Egyptians.

DID YOU KNOW?

Many Chinese cannot understand each other. They have different ways of speaking (called dialects) in different parts of the country. But today in schools all over China, the children are being taught one dialect (Mandarin), so that one day all Chinese will understand each other.

Translating computers

Computers can be used to help people of different nationalities, who do not know each others' language, talk to each other. By giving a computer a message in one language it will translate it into another specified language.

Worldwide language

English is spoken either as a first or second language in at least 45 countries. This is more than any other language. It is the language of international business and scientific conferences and is used by airtraffic controllers worldwide. In all, about one third of the world speaks it.

Earliest writing

Chinese writing has been found on pottery, and even on a tortoise shell, going back 6,000 years. Pictures made the basis for their writing, each picture showing an object or idea. Probably the earliest form of writing came from the Middle East, where Iraq and Iran are now. This region was then ruled by the Sumerians.

The most words

English has more words in it than any other language. There are about 1 million in all, a third of which are technical terms. Most people only use about 1 per cent of the words available, that is, about 10,000. William Shakespeare is reputed to have made most use of the English vocabulary.

A scientific word describing a process in the human cell is 207,000 letters long. This makes this single word equal in length to a short novel or about 80 typed sheets of A4 paper.

Many tongues

A Frenchman, named Georges Henri Schmidt, is fluent (meaning he reads and writes well) in 31 different languages.

International language

Esperanto was invented in the 1880s by a Pole, Dr Zamenhof. It was hoped that it would become the international language of Europe. It took words from many European countries and has a very easy grammar that can be learned in an hour or two.

The same language

The languages of India and Europe may originally come from just one source. Many words in different languages sound similar. For example, the word for *King* in Latin is *Rex,* in Indian, *Raj,* in Italian *Re,* in French *Roi* and in Spanish *Rey.* The original language has been named Indo-European. Basque, spoken in the French and Spanish Pyrenees, is an exception. It seems to have a different source which is still unknown.

Number of alphabets

There are 65 alphabets in use in the world today. Here are some of them:

Roman
ABCDEFGHIJKLMNOPQRS

Greek
ΑΒΓΔΕΖΗΘΙΚΛΜΝΞΟΠΡ

Russian (Cyrillic)
АЬВГДЕЖЗИЙКЛМНОП

Hebrew
מעדיף כיום דיור בשירות

Chinese
評定。因此我們制定一種申請房屋計點辦

Arabic
١٨٩٧ وصل إلى إنجلترا أنموذج

Art and entertainment

Most productive painter

Picasso, the Spanish artist who died in 1973, is estimated to have produced over 13,000 paintings, as well as a great many engravings, book illustrations and sculptures, during his long career – he lived to be 91. This means that he painted an average 3½ pictures every week of his adult life.

Most valuable painting

Leonardo da Vinci's *Mona Lisa* is probably the world's most valuable painting. It was stolen from the Louvre, Paris, in 1911, where it had hung since it was painted in 1507. It took 2 years to recover. During that time, 6 forgeries turned up in the USA, each selling for a very high price.

The oldest museum

The Ashmolean Museum in Oxford, Britain, was built in 1679.

The record of records

The *Guinness Book of Records*, first published in 1955, has been translated into 24 languages and has sold over 50 million copies worldwide.

Largest painting

The Battle of Gettysburg, is the size of 10 tennis courts. It took 2½ years to paint (1883) and measures 125 m (410 ft) by 21.1 m (70 ft). The artist was Paul Philippoteaux.

Largest art gallery

The Winter Palace and the Hermitage in Leningrad, USSR, have 322 galleries showing a total of 3 million works of art and archaeological exhibits. A walk around all the galleries is 24 km (15 miles).

Best-selling novelist

Barbara Cartland, a British authoress, has sold about 370 million copies of her romantic novels worldwide and they have been translated into 17 languages. All her books gathered together would make 5,000 piles, each as high as the Eiffel Tower.

Pop records

The Beatles were the most successful pop group of all time. They sold over 1,000 million discs and tapes. The biggest selling single was *White Christmas*, written by Irving Berlin and sung by Bing Crosby. The most successful album is *Thriller* by Michael Jackson, selling over 40 million copies.

Band Aid

On July 13th, 1985, two pop concerts took place, one in Wembley, London, and the other at the JF Kennedy Stadium, Philadelphia. Fifty well-known bands played to raise money for the starving of Africa. By the end of the year over £50 million* had been raised by the concert, a record and a book of the event.

Largest audience

In 1980 the pop star, Elton John, played in front of 400,000 people at a free summer concert in Central Park, New York.

DID YOU KNOW?

The smallest professional theatre in the world is to be found in Hamburg, Germany. *The Piccolo* seats only 30 people. The Perth Entertainment Centre, Australia, has a theatre that holds 80,000, which is a capacity over 2,500 times greater.

William Shakespeare

Shakespeare, commonly thought the world's greatest playwright, wrote 37 plays in all. The longest is *Hamlet*. The role of Hamlet is also the longest written by Shakespeare.

A night at the opera

Richard Wagner had an eccentric patron in Ludwig II, king of Bavaria. He was so impressed by Wagner's music that he built a castle (called Neuschwanstein) in Bavaria for Wagner's operas.

Expensive film

One of the most expensive films ever made was *Star Trek*, which was first shown in 1979. It cost $21 million* to make.

Amazing But True

Wolfgang Amadeus Mozart wrote about 1,000 pieces of music, including many operas and symphonies. He died aged 35, but had been composing since the age of 4. He is thought to be one of the world's greatest composers.

*See page 96

85

The world of machines

Largest and slowest

The machine that takes the Space Shuttle to its launching pad is called the *Crawler* and for a very good reason. It weighs 3,000 tonnes and travels at a maximum speed of 3 kph (2 mph). It is 40 m (130 ft) long, and 35 m (115 ft) wide.

Oldest working clock

The mechanical clock in Salisbury Cathedral, Britain, dates back to 1386. It is still in full working order, after repairs were made in 1956, some 600 years later.

Earliest steam engine

Richard Trevithick, a Cornish inventor, built the first steam engine in 1803. The first public railway was opened 23 years later between Stockton and Darlington, Britain. The engine used was designed by George Stephenson.

The sewing machine

The sewing machine was first used in France in the early 19th century. It was made of wood. Isaac Singer invented the first foot treadle machine in 1851. This became so popular that it lead to mass-production of sewing machines.

Radio fraud

In 1913, almost 50 years after the first radio transmission, an American was convicted of trying to mislead the public. He had advertised that in a few years his radio company would be able to transmit the human voice across the Atlantic to Europe. The district attorney did not believe him. Two years later a trans-Atlantic conversation took place.

A mirror on the universe

The inventor of the telescope is thought to be Roger Bacon, a 13th century monk. His instrument was first discovered in detail in 1608 by a Dutchman. Today, the most powerful telescope is in the USSR. The lens alone is 6 m (19 ft) across and weighs 70 tonnes. It can pick up the light given off from a candle 24,000 km (15,000 miles) away.

Powerful computer

One of the world's most powerful computers, the CYBER Model 205-444 system, can make 800 million calculations a second. If all the people in China could each make a calculation in a second, it would take the entire population to keep up with this computer.

Most powerful fire-engine

A fire-engine designed to tackle aircraft fires can squirt 277 gallons of foam a second out of its 2 turrets. It is the 8-wheeled Oshkosh firetruck. It could fill an olympic-sized swimming pool in only 30 minutes.

Most accurate clock

The Olsen clock in Copenhagen town hall, Denmark, will lose half a second every 300 years. It took 10 years to make. An atomic clock in the USA is accurate to within 1 second in 1,700,000 years.

Amazing But True

The fastest official record for typing is 216 words in one minute or 3½ words per second. An electronic printer in the USA can type over 3,000 times faster: that is 700,000 words a minute or 12,000 a second.

The longest cars

In 1927, 6 Bugatti 'Royales' were made in France. They were each 6.7 m (22 ft) long. A custom built Lamrooster measures 15.24 m (50 ft), has 10 wheels and a pool in the back.

World speed records

Steam locomotive	1938	202.77 kph (126 mph)
Helicopter	1978	368.00 kph (228.6 mph)
Motorcycle	1978	512.73 kph (318.6 mph)
Aircraft	1976	3,529.00 kph (2,192.9 mph)
Command Module	1969	39,897 kph (24,791.5 mph)

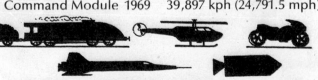

World map

Alaska

Canada

Greenland

Finland

Sweden

Norway

Iceland

Britain

Ireland

France

Portugal

Spain

United States of America

ATLANTIC OCEAN

Morocco

Western Sahara

Algeria

Bermuda

Bahamas

Cape Verde

Mauritania

Mali

Niger

Mexico

Cuba

Dominican Republic

Puerto Rico

Belize

Haiti

Gambia

Senegal

Guinea-Bissau

Nigeria

Guatemala

Honduras

Barbados

Guinea

El Salvador

Nicaragua

Guyana

Sierra Leone

Costa Rica

Venezuela

Surinam

Liberia

Benin

Panama

French Guiana

Ivory Coast

Togo

Colombia

Ghana

Gabon

PACIFIC OCEAN

Ecuador

Congo

Peru

An

Brazil

Nam

KEY TO NUMBERS

Bolivia

Paraguay

Botswana

Chile

South Af

1 Denmark
2 West Germany
3 East Germany
4 Poland
5 Czechoslovakia
6 Netherlands
7 Belgium
8 Luxembourg
9 Switzerland
10 Austria
11 Hungary
12 Romania
13 Yugoslavia
14 Bulgaria
15 Albania

Uruguay

Argentina

16 Greece
17 Syria
18 Lebanon
19 Israel
20 Jordan
21 Kuwait
22 Bahrain
23 Qatar
24 United Arab Emirates
25 Bangladesh
26 Kampuchea
27 Singapore

Falkland Islands

ARCTIC OCEAN

Union of Soviet Socialist Republics

Mongolia

N. Korea

Japan

China

S. Korea

Afghanistan

Bhutan

Taiwan

Iraq

Iran

Pakistan

Nepal

Laos

Hong Kong

Saudi
Arabia

Oman

India

Burma

Vietnam

Philippines

S. Yemen

N. Yemen

Djibouti

Thailand

Brunei

Ethiopia

Somalia

Maldives

Sri Lanka

Malaysia

Papua New Guinea

Kenya

Seychelles

Indonesia

Solomon
Islands

Tanzania

Comoros

INDIAN OCEAN

Mauritius

Fiji

Reunion

Madagascar

Australia

Mozambique

Swaziland

Lesotho

28 Burkina Faso
29 Chad
30 Cameroon
31 Central African Republic
32 Equatorial Guinea
33 Uganda
34 Rwandi
35 Burundi
36 Malawi
37 Zambia
38 Zimbabwe

New Zealand

Countries of the world facts

Country	Capital	Population	Area (sq km)
Afghanistan	Kabul	16,000,000	648,000
Albania	Tirana	2,800,000	29,000
Algeria	Algiers	19,600,000	2,382,000
Andorra	Andorra-la-Vieja	40,000	500
Angola	Luanda	7,800,000	1,247,000
Antigua and Barbuda	St John's	80,000	442
Argentina	Buenos Aires	28,200,000	2,767,000
Australia	Canberra	15,000,000	7,678,000
Austria	Vienna	7,000,000	84,000
Bahamas	Nassau	200,000	14,000
Bahrain	Manama	400,000	600
Bangladesh	Dacca	90,700,000	144,000
Barbados	Bridgetown	300,000	430
Belgium	Brussels	9,900,000	31,000
Belize	Belmopan	160,000	23,000
Benin	Porto Novo	3,600,000	113,000
Bermuda	Hamilton	60,000	50
Bhutan	Thimphu	1,300,000	47,000
Bolivia	La Paz	5,700,000	1,099,000
Botswana	Gaborone	900,000	600,000
Brazil	Brasilia	120,500,000	8,512,000
Brunei	Bandar Seri Begawan	200,000	6,000
Bulgaria	Sofia	8,900,000	111,000
Burkina Faso	Ouagadougou	6,300,000	274,000
Burma	Rangoon	34,100,000	677,000
Burundi	Bujumbura	4,200,000	28,000
Cameroon	Yaoundé	8,700,000	475,000
Canada	Ottawa	24,200,000	9,976,000
Cape Verde	Praia	300,000	4,000
Cayman Islands	Georgetown	20,000	300
Central African Republic	Bangui	2,400,000	623,000
Chad	N'Diamena	4,500,000	1,284,000
Chile	Santiago	11,300,000	757,000
China	Beijing	1,020,000,000	9,597,000
Colombia	Bogota	26,400,000	1,139,000
Comoros	Moroni	400,000	2,000
Congo	Brazzaville	1,700,000	342,000
Costa Rica	San José	2,300,000	51,000
Cuba	Havana	9,700,000	115,000
Cyprus	Nicosia	600,000	9,000
Czechoslovakia	Prague	15,300,000	128,000
Denmark	Copenhagen	5,100,000	43,000
Djibouti	Djibouti	400,000	22,000
Dominica	Roseau	70,000	751
Dominican Republic	Santo Domingo	5,600,000	49,000

Country	Capital	Population	Area (sq km)
Ecuador	Quito	8,600,000	284,000
Egypt	Cairo	43,300,000	1,001,000
El Salvador	San Salvador	4,700,000	21,000
Equatorial Guinea	Malabo	400,000	28,000
Ethiopia	Addis Ababa	31,800,000	1,222,000
Falkland Islands	Stanley	2,000	12,000
Fiji	Suva	600,000	18,000
Finland	Helsinki	4,800,000	337,000
France	Paris	55,000,000	551,000
French Guiana	Cayenne	60,000	91,000
Gabon	Libreville	700,000	268,000
Gambia	Banjul	600,000	11,000
Germany, East	Berlin	16,700,000	108,000
Germany, West	Bonn	61,700,000	249,000
Ghana	Accra	11,800,000	239,000
Greece	Athens	9,700,000	132,000
Greenland	Godthaab	50,000	2,186,000
Grenada	St George's	100,000	344
Guadeloupe	Basse-Terre	350,000	2,000
Guatemala	Guatemala City	7,500,000	109,000
Guinea	Conakry	5,600,000	246,000
Guinea-Bissau	Bissau	800,000	36,000
Guyana	Georgetown	800,000	215,000
Haiti	Port-au-Prince	5,100,000	28,000
Honduras	Tegucigalpa	3,800,000	112,000
Hong Kong	Hong Kong	5,200,000	1,000
Hungary	Budapest	10,700,000	93,000
Iceland	Reykjavik	200,000	103,000
India	New Delhi	729,000,000	3,288,000
Indonesia	Jakarta	160,000,000	1,904,000
Iran	Tehrán	40,000,000	1,648,000
Iraq	Baghdad	13,500,000	435,000
Ireland	Dublin	3,400,000	70,000
Israel	Jerusalem	4,000,000	21,000
Italy	Rome	56,200,000	301,000
Ivory Coast	Abidjan	8,500,000	322,000
Jamaica	Kingston	2,200,000	11,000
Japan	Tokyo	117,600,000	372,000
Jordan	Amman	3,400,000	98,000
Kampuchea	Phnom Penh	7,100,000	181,000
Kenya	Nairobi	17,400,000	583,000
Kiribati	Tarawa	60,000	717
Korea, North	Pyongyang	18,700,000	121,000
Korea, South	**Seoul**	38,900,000	98,000
Kuwait	Kuwait	1,500,000	18,000

Country	Capital	Population	Area (sq km)
Laos	Vientiane	3,500,000	237,000
Lebanon	Beirut	2,700,000	10,000
Lesotho	Maseru	1,400,000	30,000
Liberia	Monrovia	1,900,000	111,000
Libya	Tripoli	3,100,000	1,760,000
Liechtenstein	Vaduz	30,000	160
Luxembourg	Luxembourg	400,000	3,000
Madagascar	Antananarivo	9,000,000	587,000
Malawi	Lilongwe	6,200,000	118,000
Malaysia	Kuala Lumpur	14,200,000	330,000
Maldives	Malé	200,000	300
Mali	Bamako	6,900,000	1,240,000
Malta	Valletta	400,000	300
Martinique	Fort-de-France	300,000	1,000
Mauritania	Nouakchott	1,600,000	1,031,000
Mauritius	Port Louis	1,000,000	2,000
Mexico	Mexico City	71,200,000	1,973,000
Monaco	Monaco	30,000	2
Mongolia	Ulaanbaatar	1,700,000	1,567,000
Morocco	Rabat	20,900,000	447,000
Mozambique	Maputo	12,500,000	783,000
Namibia	Windhoek	1,000,000	824,000
Nauru	Nauru	7,000	21
Nepal	Katmandu	15,000,000	141,000
Netherlands	Amsterdam	14,200,000	37,000
New Zealand	Wellington	3,300,000	269,000
Nicaragua	Managua	2,800,000	130,000
Niger	Niamey	5,700,000	1,267,000
Nigeria	Lagos	87,600,000	925,000
Norway	Oslo	4,100,000	324,000
Oman	Muscat	900,000	212,000
Pakistan	Islamabad	84,500,000	804,000
Panama	Panama City	1,900,000	77,000
Papua New Guinea	Port Moresby	3,100,000	462,000
Paraguay	Asunción	3,100,000	407,000
Peru	Lima	17,000,000	1,285,000
Philippines	Manila	49,600,000	300,000
Poland	Warsaw	35,900,000	313,000
Portugal	Lisbon	10,000,000	92,000
Puerto Rico	San Juan	3,700,000	9,000
Qatar	Doha	200,000	11,000
Reunion	Saint-Denis	500,000	3,000
Romania	Bucharest	22,500,000	238,000
Rwanda	Kigali	5,300,000	26,000
St Christopher-Nevis	Basseterre	50,000	300
St Lucia	Castries	100,000	600
St Vincent	Kingstown	100,000	389

Country	Capital	Population	Area (sq km)
San Marino	San Marino	20,000	61
São Tomé and Principe	São Tomé	100,000	1,000
Saudi Arabia	Riyadh	9,300,000	2,150,000
Senegal	Dakar	5,900,000	196,000
Seychelles	Victoria	60,000	440
Sierra Leone	Freetown	3,600,000	72,000
Singapore	Singapore	2,400,000	600
Solomon Islands	Honiara	200,000	28,000
Somalia	Mogadiscio	4,400,000	638,000
South Africa	Pretoria	29,500,000	1,221,000
Spain	Madrid	38,000,000	505,000
Sri Lanka	Colombo	15,000,000	66,000
Sudan	Khartoum	19,200,000	2,506,000
Surinam	Paramaribo	400,000	163,000
Swaziland	Mbabane	600,000	17,000
Sweden	Stockholm	8,300,000	450,000
Switzerland	Berne	6,500,000	41,000
Syria	Damascus	9,300,000	185,000
Taiwan	Taipei	18,300,000	36,000
Tanzania	Dodoma	19,100,000	945,000
Thailand	Bangkok	48,000,000	514,000
Togo	Lomé	2,700,000	56,000
Tonga	Nuku'alofa	100,000	800
Trinidad and Tobago	Port-of-Spain	1,200,000	5,000
Tunisia	Tunis	6,500,000	164,000
Turkey	Ankara	45,500,000	781,000
Tuvalu	Funafuti	10,000	26
Uganda	Kampala	13,000,000	236,000
USSR	Moscow	275,000,000	22,402,000
United Arab Emirates	Abu Dhabi	1,100,000	87,000
United Kingdom	London	56,000,000	244,000
USA	Washington DC	235,000,000	9,363,000
Uruguay	Montevideo	2,900,000	176,000
Vanuatu	Vila	100,000	15,000
Vatican City		1,000	0.4
Venezuela	Caracas	15,400,000	912,000
Vietnam	Hanoi	55,700,000	330,000
Virgin Islands	Road Town	10,000	100
Western Sahara	El Aaiún	120,000	267,800
Western Samoa	Apia	200,000	3,000
Yemen, North	Saná	7,300,000	195,000
Yemen, South	Aden	2,000,000	333,000
Yugoslavia	Belgrade	22,300,000	256,000
Zaire	Kinshasa	29,800,000	2,345,000
Zambia	Lusaka	5,800,000	753,000
Zimbabwe	Harare	7,200,000	391,000

Index

*

Currency conversion chart (correct on July 16th, 1990)

	US $	Sing. $	NZ $	Aust. $	Can.$	£ Sterling
US $	1.0	1.82	1.68	1.28	1.16	0.56
Singapore $1	0.55	1.0	0.93	0.70	0.64	0.31
New Zealand $1	0.59	1.08	1.0	0.76	0.69	0.33
Australian $1	0.78	1.42	1.32	1.0	0.90	0.43
Canadian $1	0.87	1.57	1.46	1.11	1.0	0.48
£1 Sterling	1.80	3.27	3.03	2.30	2.08	1.0

WEATHER FACTS

Anita Ganeri

Consultant: Roger Hunt, London Weather Centre

CONTENTS

Illustrated by Tony Gibson

**Additional illustrations by
Martin Newton and Ian Jackson**

Designed by Teresa Foster

Additional designs by Tony Gibson

Additional research by Chris Rice

What is weather?

Weather everywhere

The four main ingredients which cause weather are the Sun, the atmosphere, water vapour and the wind. These all work together, spreading the Sun's heat around the world and making clouds, rain and snow. Weather is an endless cycle of events. It happens all around us all the time fitting together like a jigsaw.

Where it happens

The atmosphere is like a giant blanket of air around the Earth. It is divided into layers. Weather happens in the troposphere, the layer directly above the ground. Above the Equator the troposphere is about 16 km (10 miles) deep. Mount Everest, the highest point on Earth, reaches about half way up the troposphere.

Heavy air

The air presses down all over the Earth. This is called air or atmospheric pressure. The weight of air pressing down on each 1 sq m (10 sq ft) of the Earth's surface is greater than that of a large elephant. Air also

presses down on our bodies but we do not feel it because breathing balances out the effect. Air pressure is greatest at ground level and gets less the higher up you go. Aircraft are specially pressurized so people can breathe.

Barometers

Barometers measure air pressure. On an aneroid barometer a needle on a dial moves as the air pressure changes. Pressure is measured in millibars (mb). At sea level pressure is usually between 900-1050 mb. Pressure can also be measured in mm (in) of mercury with a mercury barometer.

Amazing But True

In 1654 Otto von Guericke, a German scientist, showed just how strong air pressure can be. He fitted two halves of a hollow sphere, about 56 cm (22 in) across, together so tightly that they were completely airtight. Then he pumped all the air out of them. The air pressure outside was so strong that it took 16 horses to pull the two halves apart.

Air masses

Air masses are huge masses of air which are warm, cold, dry or moist depending on the nature of the land or sea they pass over. They cover vast areas, often some 1,000,000 sq km (386,000 sq miles), about the same size as Egypt. Air masses move over the Earth's surface and help spread the Sun's heat around the world.

Highs and lows

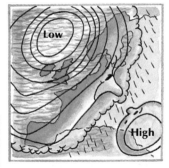

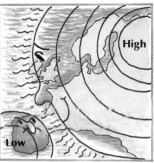

Air masses

Polar continental · Polar maritime · Tropical maritime · Tropical continental

Air masses are named after the type of climate they come from. There are four main kinds:

Polar continental (cP)
Forms over very cold land like North Canada. Cold and dry in winter, warm in summer.

Polar maritime (mP)
Forms over cold Northern seas like the Arctic Ocean. Cool and showery.

Tropical continental (cT)
Comes from warm inland places like the Sahara Desert. Is hot and dry.

Tropical maritime (mT)
Forms over warm oceans near the Equator. It is warm, moist and brings unsettled weather.

Pressure is different all over the world. Lows are areas of low pressure with the lowest pressure at the centre. Highs are areas of high pressure with the highest pressure at the centre. The way these move from day to day causes the changes in the weather. Lows usually bring wet, cloudy weather. Highs bring sunnier, dry weather.

Fronts

Boundaries between air masses are called fronts. Near fronts the weather can be very unsettled, with rain and clouds. Some cold fronts cause lines of violent storms, as long as 800 km (500 miles). The three types of front are warm, cold and occluded. An occluded front is where a cold front overtakes a warm one.

Finding the lows

If you stand with your back to the wind in the northern hemisphere the nearest low will be on your left. In the southern hemisphere it is on your right.

cold front · cold air · warm air · warm front · cold air

The Sun
Energetic Sun

Highest recorded temperatures		
Africa	58°C	Azizia, Libya
America	57°C	Death Valley, California
Asia	54°C	Tirat Tsvi, Israel
Australia	53°C	Cloncurry, Queensland
Europe	50°C	Seville, Spain
Antarctica	14°C	Esperanza, Palmer

All the Earth's heat and light comes from the Sun. More heat and light reaches the Earth from the Sun in one minute than the whole world can produce in a year. Sunlight travels at about 300,000 km (186,000 miles) per second. It takes about 8½ minutes to reach the Earth.

Life support

The Sun keeps the temperature of most of the Earth's surface at −51°C to 49°C (−60°F to 120°F). Most living things can only survive at 0°C to 49°C (32°F to 120°F). If the amount of sunlight reaching the Earth was cut by a tenth, the oceans would turn to ice and life on Earth would die.

Effect on the weather

The Sun is the key to the world's weather. Its rays filter through the atmosphere and warm the Earth's surface which, in turn, heats the air above. The Equator is hot because the Sun shines directly overhead. The Poles are cold because the rays hit the Earth at wider angles.

DID YOU KNOW?

The light given off by a piece of the Sun's surface the size of a postage stamp is more than 500 60-watt light bulbs. It could light all the rooms in 48 average-sized homes.

The snug Earth

The Earth absorbs sunlight and then releases it into the air again as heat. The heat is trapped by water vapour and clouds in the atmosphere and reflected back to Earth. The atmosphere acts like an enormous blanket around the Earth, keeping in the warmth.

Cold mountains

People used to think that the closer you went to the Sun, the hotter it would be. But as hot air rises it expands and cools, so the higher you go the colder it is. Air cools by 3°C (5.5°F) for every 305 m (1,000 ft) it rises. This is why the tops of mountains are cold.

100

Lowest recorded temperatures

Antarctica	−88°C	Vostok
Asia	−68°C	Oymyakon, USSR
America	−63°C	Snag, Yukon
Europe	−55°C	Ust'Schchugor, USSR
Africa	−24°C	Ilfrane, Morocco
Australia	−22°C	Charlotte Pass, NSW

Solar power

Solar panels are used to collect the Sun's heat. Water in them absorbs the heat and is used to warm homes. Electricity can also be made from sunlight. In 1982 the car *The Quiet Achiever* was driven right across Australia on sunshine power alone.

Hottest and coldest

At Dallol, Ethiopia the mean (average) shade temperature over a year is 34.4°C (94°F), making it the hottest place in the world. The coldest place in the world is Vostok in Antarctica where the mean temperature over a year is a freezing −57.8°C (−72°F).

Sunspots

Sunspots are dark patches on the Sun's surface. A single spot may be 8 times the Earth's diameter. They become very active every 11 years. Meteorologists think that sunspot activity may alter weather patterns by affecting the Earth's magnetic fields.

Thermometers

Thermometers are used to measure temperature. They are placed in the shade, 1.5 m (5 ft) off the ground. In direct sunshine and on the ground, the temperature recorded may be much higher than that off the ground.

Amazing But True

Solar ponds are lakes of salty water which collect the Sun's heat in their deepest, saltiest layers. The temperature can reach boiling point.

Scientists in New Mexico, USA proved this by boiling eggs in a solar pond. The eggs only took about five minutes to cook.

Water on the move

The world's water

About 70% of the Earth is covered with water. Most of this lies in the oceans. The Pacific Ocean alone covers almost half the world. Much of the rest of the water is in the ice sheets, glaciers and underground.

The water cycle

No new water is ever made. The rain you see has fallen millions of times before. In the water cycle the water on the Earth is used again and again. The Sun heats the oceans and lakes and millions of gallons of water rise into the air as invisible water vapour.

This is called evaporation. As the vapour rises, it cools and turns back into liquid water. This is called condensation. It falls as rain and snow and is carried back to the ocean by rivers and streams. Then the cycle begins all over again.

Water's disguises

There are 3 forms of water in the air:
1 The gas water vapour.
2 Liquid water droplets.
3 Solid ice crystals.
It changes from one form to another by evaporation, freezing, melting and condensation.

Watery air

The amount of water vapour in the air is called humidity. All air contains some water vapour but the amount varies greatly. Warm air can hold more vapour than cold air. In the Tropics the air is hot and sticky and contains nearly as much water vapour as the air in a sauna. It can be very uncomfortable.

DID YOU KNOW?

If all the water in the air fell at the same time, it would cover the whole Earth with 25 mm (1 in) of rain. This amount of rain would fill enough buckets to reach from the Earth to the Sun 57 million times.

Dew point

As air cools at night there is a point when it cannot hold any more water vapour and condensation begins. This is called the dew point and dew forms on the ground. It evaporates in the morning when the air warms up.

Dew traps

Farmers in Lanzarotte, Canary Islands, collect dew to water their crops. The dew traps look like moon craters, 3 m (10 ft) wide and 2 m (6 ft) deep. A layer of volcanic ash inside makes a good surface for condensation. Vines planted in the craters can live on the dew if it does not rain.

Rivers in the sea

Oceans have a great effect on climate. They absorb the Sun's heat and spread it around the world in currents. These are huge rivers in the sea driven by the winds. Warm and cold currents heat or cool the air above them causing hotter or cooler types of weather.

The oceans

The oceans supply most of the water for the water cycle. In a year up to 2,000 mm (79 in) of water evaporates from the Pacific and the Indian Oceans. It would take over a million years for the oceans' total water supply to pass through the air.

The West Wind Drift carries over 2,000 times more water than the Amazon, the world's largest river. It flows three times as fast as the Gulf Stream and about 2½ times faster than the fastest man can swim.

The Gulf Stream

The warm Gulf Stream, one of the strongest currents, speeds east across the Atlantic at 178 km (111 miles) a day. It then turns north and divides, bringing mild weather to Europe. New York is only 160 km (100 miles) north of Lisbon in Portugal but in January it is cold at −1°C (31°F) while Lisbon is sunny at 10°C (50°F).

Clouds

How clouds form

Clouds form when warm air rises and cools down enough for some of the water vapour in it to condense into tiny water droplets or ice crystals. Billions of these make up a cloud. Water vapour can also condense on to smoke or dust specks in the air.

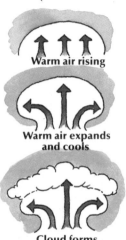

Warm air rising

Warm air expands and cools

Cloud forms

Two basic shapes

There are two basic cloud shapes caused by the two ways in which air can rise. 'Heap' (cumuliform) clouds form when bubbles of warm air rise quickly and then cool. 'Layer' (stratiform) clouds form when a large, spreading mass of air rises very slowly.

Amazing But True

The tallest cloud is the giant cumulonimbus. It can reach a height of 18 km (11 miles) which is twice as high as Mount Everest and can hold more than ½ million tonnes of water.

Water music

People in Chile's dry Atacama Desert collect water from sea fog. They use fog harps which are wooden frames strung with nylon threads. Water from the fog condenses on to the threads. More than 18 litres (32 pints) of water can be collected on 1 sq m (3 sq ft) of thread in a day.

Fog

Fog is really low cloud which forms when air near the ground cools. Sea fog forms when warm air from the land flows over cold seas. In the Arctic fog can rise up from the sea like steam rising from hot water. It is called sea smoke.

Fog danger

Fog reduces visibility and causes accidents on land and at sea. In 1962 two trains crashed in thick fog in London. 90 people were killed and many more injured.

DID YOU KNOW?

For centuries sailors lost at sea have used clouds to guide them to land. Fleecy clouds on the horizon often form above islands.

Cloud messengers

There are three families of clouds. They were given Latin names by Luke Howard in 1804. They are cirrus ('curl of hair'), cumulus ('heap') and stratus ('layer'). There are 10 main types of clouds made up of combinations of these families. Clouds are also grouped by their height above the ground. Each cloud carries a message about the weather to come so weather men use clouds to help them make forecasts.

Cirrus

High, ice-crystal clouds which look like wispy curls of hair. Often signs of bad weather to come.

Cirrostratus

Sheets of thin, milk-coloured cloud which form high up and often bring rain within 24 hours.

Altostratus

Layers of thin, grey cloud which can grow into rain clouds. Often form haloes round the Sun.

Stratocumulus

Uneven rolls or patches of cloud across the sky. Usually a sign that drier weather is on the way.

Cumulus

Clearly defined puffs of fluffy cloud like cauliflowers. They appear in sunny, summer skies.

Cirrocumulus

Often called a 'mackerel sky' – the ripples of cloud look like fish scales. Unsettled weather.

Altocumulus

Fluffy waves of grey cloud which can bring showers or break up to give sunny periods.

Nimbostratus

Thick, dark grey masses of cloud which bring rain or snow. 'Nimbus' means rain in Latin.

Stratus

Low, grey blanket of cloud which often brings drizzle. It can cover high ground and cause hill fog.

Cumulonimbus

Towering clouds which usually bring thunderstorms with rain, snow or hail.

Rainfall

Out of the clouds

Raindrops form in clouds when tiny water droplets join together or larger ice crystals melt. A raindrop must contain as many as 1,000 droplets for it to be heavy enough to fall. When water falls as rain or snow it is called precipitation.

Greatest average annual rainfalls		
Continent	MM	Place
Oceania (Pacific islands)	11,684	Mt Wai-'ale-'ale, Hawaii
Asia	11,430	Cherrapunji, India
Africa	10,277	Debundseha, Cameroon
S. America	8,991	Quibdo, Colombia
N. America	6,655	Henderson Lake, British Colombia
Europe	4,648	Crkvice, Yugoslavia
Australia	4,496	Tully, Queensland

Raindrops and drizzle

Raindrops are usually about 1.5 mm (0.06 in) round. They never grow bigger than 5 mm (0.2 in) which is about the size of a pea. Drops less than 0.5 mm (0.02 in) round are called drizzle. Raindrops are not tear-shaped, as is often thought, but look like flat-bottomed circles.

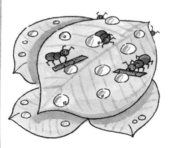

From dry to worse

From 1570-1971 Calama, Chile held the record for being the driest place in the world. It had had no rain at all for 400 years. But on 10 February 1972 torrential rain fell causing terrible floods. The whole town was surrounded by water and its electricity supply was cut off. Many buildings were badly damaged.

Least average annual rainfalls		
Continent	MM	Place
S. America	0.8	Arica, Chile
Africa	2.5	Wadi Halfa, Sudan
N. America	30.5	Bataques, Mexico
Asia	45.7	Aden, South Yemen
Australia	119.3	Millers Creek
Europe	162.5	Astrakhan, USSR
Oceania	226.0	Puako, Hawaii

Greatest observed rainfalls		
Time	MM	Place
1 min	38	Barst, Guardeloupe
15 min	198	Plumb Point, Jamaica
12 hours	1,340	Belouve, Reunion
24 hours	1,869	Cilaos, Reunion
1 month	9,299	Cherrapunji, India
1 year	26,459	Cherrapunji, India

Most rainy days

Amazing But True

On 9 February 1859 a shower of fish fell in Glamorgan, Wales. They covered an area about the size of three tennis courts laid end to end. No one knew where they came from.

Smell of rain

Many people claim to be able to smell rain. This may be because our sense of smell is keener when the air is moist and also because of the gases given off by wet soil and plants.

Rain forests

In the tropical rain forests of South America it rains nearly every day. Each year at least 2,030 mm (80 in) and as much as 3,810 mm (150 in) of rain can fall. The air is always moist and sticky.

Rain gauge

Rain gauges measure the depth of rain which would cover the ground if none of it drained away or evaporated. The simplest type is a funnel connected to a tank which collects and measures the day's rainfall.

Rain does not fall evenly over the Earth. Mount Wai-'ale-'ale in Hawaii is the wettest place in the world. It has rain for about 335 days of the year. The annual rainfall is 11,684 mm (460 in) which would cover six people standing on each other's shoulders.

Dust Bowl

Drought is caused by a lack of rain. The Dust Bowl in America was created by years of drought from 1930-1940. The soil was so dry it was blown away by the wind and farmers were ruined. The Dust Bowl reached from Texas right to the Canadian border.

107

Ice and snow

What is snow?

Snow crystals form when water freezes on to ice pellets in a cloud, making them bigger. As they fall through the cloud they collide with other snow crystals and become snowflakes. Snow often melts as it passes through warmer air and falls as rain.

World snowfall records		
City	Date	Amount
London	19 January 1881	4.5 m snow drifts
New York	6 February 1978	65 cm snow
Sydney	28 June 1836	Only snow on record
Jordan	2 March 1980	38 cm in Amman
Ireland	1 April 1917	25 m drifts

Snowball fight

Snow is more likely the higher you go. Some mountains are always covered in snow. In November 1958 rain fell in the New York streets while security guards on top of the Empire State Building enjoyed a snowball fight.

Snow wonder

Most snow crystals have six sides. Billions and billions have fallen to Earth but no two have ever been seen to be identical. The shape of the crystals depends on the air temperature. In colder air, needle and rod shapes form. Complicated shapes form in warmer air.

Greatest snowfall

The most snow to fall in a year was at Paradise, Mount Rainier, USA from 1971-1972. Some 31,102 mm (1,224 in) of snow fell, enough to reach a third of the way up the Statue of Liberty in New York.

Palace of ice

In 1740 the Empress of Russia built a palace of ice as a home for a newly-married prince who had disobeyed her. Everything in it was carved from ice, even the pillows on the bed. Luckily for the prince his chilly home melted in the spring.

DID YOU KNOW?

Metal pipes often burst when the water inside them turns to ice. This is because water expands when it freezes. It also becomes lighter. If ice did not float on water the seas would gradually turn to ice and no life would be able to survive on Earth.

What is hail?

Hail only falls from cumulonimbus clouds. Ice crystals are tossed up and down in the cloud as many as 25 times. Water freezes on to the crystals in layers, like the skins of an onion, until they are heavy enough to fall as hailstones. They are usually about the size and shape of peas but many unusual stones have fallen.

In 1930 five German pilots bailed out of their aircraft into a thundercloud over the Rhön mountains in Germany. They became the centres of hailstones and were bounced up and down in the cloud. Covered by layers of ice, they eventually fell frozen to the ground. Only one of the pilots survived.

Lucky escape

The sea between Denmark and Sweden can freeze over and the ice can be strong enough for cars to cross it. In 1716 the King of Sweden led his army over the ice to invade Denmark. The lucky Danes were saved by the ice melting.

Hail damage

Hail can badly damage crops and houses. Hailstones as big as cricket balls fell in Dallas, USA in May 1926 causing $2 million of damage in just 15 minutes. Farmers in Italy often shoot firework rockets into clouds to try to shatter the hailstones.

Jack Frost

At night the ground cools and, in turn, cools the air around it. If the temperature falls below freezing point dew freezes and is called frost. Hoar frost often forms around keyholes and delicate fern frost on windows.

The biggest hailstone

A hailstone the size of a melon fell in Coffeyville, Kansas, USA on 3 September 1970. It weighed 750 g (1.67 lb) and was 44.5 cm (17.5 in) round.

Thunder and lightning

Thunderstorms

Thunderstorms usually happen when the air is warm and humid. Huge cumulonimbus clouds form in the sky and gusty winds begin to blow. A thunderstorm often lasts for less than an hour but it produces the most dramatic type of weather.

Storm survival

Lightning always takes the quickest path to the ground. Tall trees and buildings are most at risk. Very few people are struck by lightning but it is dangerous to stand near a tree in a storm. It is safest to be in a car as the lightning will go into the ground through the rubber tyres.

DID YOU KNOW?

There are about 16 million thunderstorms a year throughout the world. About 1,800 storms rage at any moment day or night.

Lightning

Electricity builds up in a thunder cloud and is released as a brilliant flash of lightning. A 'leader' stroke zig-zags to the ground. It forms a narrow path for the 'return' stroke (the one we see) to race up. Lightning can go from clouds to the ground or from cloud to cloud.

Thunder

Lightning can heat the air in its path to 30,000°C (54,000°F) which is 5 times hotter than the Sun's surface. This air expands at great speed and causes the booming noise we call thunder. Thunder can be heard at least 16 km (10 miles) away.

1, 2, 3, 4, 5 . . .

Lightning and thunder happen at exactly the same time but you see lightning first because light travels faster than sound. If you hear a thunderclap 5 seconds after you see a flash, the storm is about 2 km (1.2 miles) away.

Unlucky strike

Lightning has hit the Empire State Building in New York as much as 12 times in 20 minutes and as often as 500 times a year. Most tall buildings have lightning conductors to carry the electricity safely to the ground.

Lightning birth?

Lightning may have been one of the causes of life on Earth. Scientists in the USA sent artificial lightning through a mixture of gases similar to those in the atmosphere. Amino acids formed which are believed to be the basic ingredients found in all forms of life on Earth.

Types of lightning

Forked............many branches
Pearl necklace.....points of extra brightness
Ribbon ....follows a very bent path
Rocket............travels very slowly
Sheet ....flashes from behind a cloud
Streak.............one main stroke and lots of smaller shoots

Flash lighting

There are about 6,000 flashes of lightning every minute in the world. If the electricity from these could be collected and stored it would be enough to light every home in Britain and France for ever.

Most thundery place

Bogor in Java has at least 220 thundery days a year and has had as many as 322. It has at least 25 severe storms a year with lightning often striking a small area every 30 seconds for up to half an hour.

Ball lightning

'Fireballs' may or may not exist. There have been many reports of pear-shaped balls of fire floating into houses and then exploding. In 1980 a motorist in Britain saw a flashing ball of fire pass his car. It then exploded quite harmlessly.

Lightning speed

Lightning can travel at a speed of up to 140,000 km/s (87,000 miles/s) on its return journey. A rocket travelling at this speed would reach the Moon in 2½ seconds.

Amazing But True

The only person to survive being struck by lightning seven times was an American, Roy C. Sullivan. He lost his big toenail in 1942, his eyebrows in 1969 and had his hair set on fire twice. The other times he suffered slight burns.

World winds ... 1

What is wind?

Wind is simply moving air. The Sun heats up some parts of the Earth more than others and the wind spreads this heat more evenly around the world. The map shows the main world and local winds.

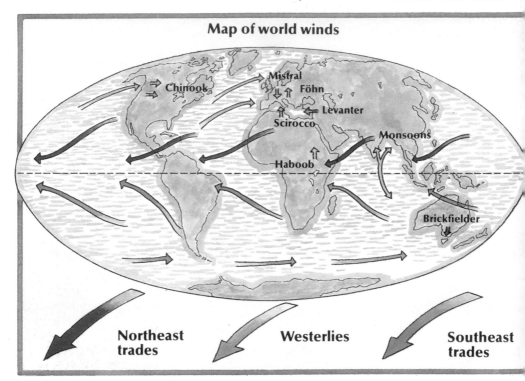

Map of world winds

Chinook

Mistral

Föhn

Levanter

Scirocco

Monsoons

Haboob

Brickfielder

Northeast trades

Westerlies

Southeast trades

How does it blow?

Air moves because of differences in pressure around the world. Warm air is light and rises leaving an area of low pressure as at the hot Equator. Cold air is heavier and sinks, causing high pressure, as at the icy Poles. Air flows from high to low pressure but it does not flow in a straight line from the Poles to the Equator. It is swung sidewards by the Earth's spin.

In a spin

The Earth spins on its axis and this affects the direction of the wind. In the northern hemisphere winds are swung to the right, and in the southern to the left. This is called the Coriolis effect.

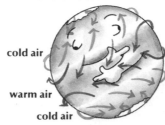

cold air

warm air

cold air

DID YOU KNOW?

In the northern hemisphere winds flow from west to east. This means that an aircraft flying from New York to London could arrive about ½ hour early because it has the wind behind it. But it could be delayed by ½ hour on the way back when flying into the wind.

Trade winds

The trade winds are steady winds flowing towards the Equator. In the 18th century sailing ships used them as guides for crossing the Atlantic Ocean. Columbus might never have discovered America in 1492 without the trade winds' help.

Jet streams

Jet streams are very strong winds blowing about 10 km (6 miles) above the Earth. They can be up to 4,000 km (2,500 miles) long but no more than 500 km (310 miles) wide. They were not discovered until World War II when pilots found their air speed reduced when they were flying against the jet stream.

Sea breezes

On a hot, sunny day the land heats up more quickly than the sea. Because of this air rises over the land and cool sea breezes rush in to replace it.

By evening sea breezes can reach 200 km (322 miles) inland. At night land cools down more quickly than the sea so the breeze blows out from land to sea.

Local winds

Winds affect the weather and are given special names in many parts of the world.

Brickfielder	Very hot NE summer wind that blows dust and sand across Australia.
Chinook	Warm, dry wind of the Rocky Mountains, USA. Welcomed by cattlemen because it can remove snow cover very quickly. Named after a local Indian tribe.
Föhn	Warm, dry European wind that flows down the side of mountains.
Haboob	The Arabic name for a violent wind which raises sandstorms, especially in North Africa.
Levanter	Pleasant, moist E wind that brings mild weather to the Mediterranean.
Mistral	Violent, dry, cold, NW wind that blows along the coasts of Spain and France.
Scirocco	Hot, dry S wind that blows across North Africa from the Sahara. Becomes very hot and sticky as it reaches the sea.

Amazing But True

Rising air currents called thermals can delay the fall of a parachutist. On 26 July 1959 an American pilot ejected from his plane at 14,400 m (47,000 ft) and took 40 minutes to fall through a thunder cloud instead of the expected 11 minutes.

World Winds . . . 2

The Beaufort Scale

The Beaufort Scale was invented in 1805 by Admiral Beaufort to estimate wind speed.

The original scale was for use at sea but it has been adapted for use on land.

The Beaufort Scale for use on land			
Force	Strength	Kph	Effect
0	Calm	0-1	Smoke rises vertically
1	Light air	1-5	Smoke drifts slowly
2	Light breeze	6-11	Wind felt on face; leaves rustle
3	Gentle breeze	12-19	Twigs move; light flag unfurls
4	Moderate breeze	20-29	Dust and paper blown about; small branches move
5	Fresh breeze	30-39	Wavelets on inland water; small trees move
6	Strong breeze	40-50	Large branches sway; umbrellas turn inside out
7	Near gale	51-61	Whole trees sway; difficult to walk against wind
8	Gale	62-74	Twigs break off trees; walking very hard
9	Strong gale	75-87	Chimney pots, roof tiles and branches blown down
10	Storm	88-101	Trees uprooted; severe damage to buildings
11	Violent storm	102-117	Widespread damage to buildings
12	Hurricane	Over 119	Devastation

DID YOU KNOW?

A wind that blows as fast as the fastest man can run (43 kph/27 mph), is only a 'strong breeze' on the Beaufort Scale. A wind as fast as a running cheetah (113 kph/70 mph), the world's fastest animal, registers as a 'storm'.

Blowing in the wind

Wind speed and strength must be allowed for when new buildings are designed. The bridge over the Tacoma Narrows in the USA shook so violently in strong winds that it was nicknamed 'Galloping Gertie'. It eventually collapsed during a severe storm.

Windblown

Ship designers are now going back to building sailing ships to take advantage of the wind. In August 1980, a Japanese tanker, the *Shinaltoku Maru*, was launched. As well as an engine it had two square sails, controlled by computer.

Wind chill is the cooling effect of the wind on the skin. The stronger the wind the more heat is lost from the body and the colder a person feels. If human skin were exposed to winds of 48 kph (30 mph) in a temperature of −34°C (−30°F) it would freeze solid in 30 seconds.

Wind power

Windmills were once used to grind wheat to make flour. Today they are being used to generate electricity. The windmill at Tvind, Denmark is over 50 m (164 ft) high with three blades, each weighing over 5 tonnes. It can produce enough electricity to light up about 120 homes.

Windiest place

The windiest place in the world is the George V Coast in Antarctica. Here gales of 320 kph (200 mph) have been recorded.

Highest recorded gust

On 12 April 1934 a gust of wind blowing at 371 kph (231 mph) was recorded at Mount Washington, USA. This is some 251 kph (155 mph) stronger than Beaufort Scale 12, three times as strong as a hurricane.

Wind palace

The Wind Palace in Jaipur, India was specially built in the 1760s by the king so that the wind would cool it naturally. The palace is little more than a screen with balconies. The ladies of the court could sit behind these and watch the busy city down below.

Hat trick

Because wind funnels through mountains it may be stronger in a pass than on a peak. At Pali Lookout near Honolulu, a sightseer can throw his hat over the cliff and the wind will immediately throw it back .

Hurricanes

Tropical terrors

Hurricanes begin over warm, tropical oceans. They are like giant spinning wheels of storm clouds, wind and rain and can be up to 500 km (310 miles) across with winds whirling at up to 300 kph (190 mph). They sweep westwards over warm tropical seas, dying down when they reach land.

Stormy eyes

A hurricane has a centre or 'eye'. It can be up to 32 km (20 miles) across. Here the weather is surprisingly calm with low winds and clear skies. As the 'eye' passes overhead there is a lull in the storm for a few minutes or at the most a few hours.

Hurricane map with local names

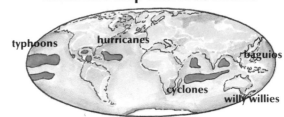

typhoons   hurricanes   baguios   cyclones   willy willies

Hurricanes turn anti-clockwise north of the Equator and clockwise to the south.

I name you . . .

Hurricanes were first given names in the 19th century by Clement Wragge, an Australian weather man. Nicknamed 'Wet Wragge', he used the names of people he had quarrelled with for very violent storms. Today an alphabetical list of names is drawn up each year for the coming year's hurricanes.

DID YOU KNOW?

If all the energy from one hurricane in a single day could be converted into electricity, it would be enough to supply the whole of the USA for three years. This is equivalent to the amount of energy needed to power 1,095 cars an incredible 36,000 times around the world.

5 of the worst recent hurricanes

Name	Date		Location	Effect
Unnamed	November	1970	Bangladesh	1 million dead
Tracey	December	1974	Darwin, Australia	90% of people homeless
David	August	1979	Dominica, W. Indies	2,000 dead; 20,000 homeless
Frederic	August	1979	Alabama, USA	£250 million damage
Allen	August	1980	Haiti	½ million homeless

Tornadoes

Terrible twisters

Tornadoes are funnel-shaped storms which twist as hot air spins upwards. At the centre winds can reach 644 kph (400 mph). Tornadoes leapfrog across land causing great damage when they touch the ground. They can suck up anything in their path, even people. Mid-West America has the most tornadoes.

Picked clean

Several chickens had all their feathers plucked off by a tornado in Bedfordshire, England in May 1950 . . . and they survived!

Tornado on tour

On 26 May 1917, a single tornado sped 471 km (293 miles) across Texas, USA. It travelled at 88-120 kph (55-75 mph) for about 7 hours and 20 minutes.

Most destructive

Tornadoes are much smaller than hurricanes but much more violent. The tornado which hit Missouri, USA in March 1925 was only 274 m (900 ft) across. It killed 800 people and uprooted trees, swept cars over rooftops and hurled aside trains.'

Amazing But True

On 4 September 1981 a tornado hit Ancona in Italy. It lifted a baby asleep in its pram 15 m (50 ft) into the air and set it down safely 100 m (328 ft) away. The baby was still sleeping soundly!

Train thief

A tornado in Minnesota, USA in 1931 lifted an 83-tonne train 25 m (80 ft) into the air and dropped it in a ditch. Many of its 117 passengers died.

Highest waterspout

Waterspouts are like tornadoes but these funnels of water form over sea. The highest seen was in 1898 in Australia. It was 1,528 m (5,015 ft) high and 3.1 m (10 ft) across.

Climate and the seasons

What is climate?

Climate is the usual pattern of weather a place has measured over a very long time. How hot or cold a place is depends on how far north or south of the Equator it is (its latitude). Ocean currents, winds and mountains also affect climate.

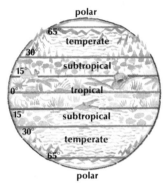

Climates of the world

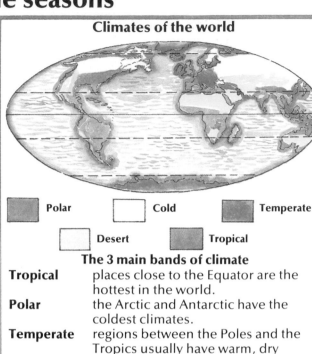

Polar □ Cold □ Temperate

□ Desert □ Tropical

The 3 main bands of climate

Tropical places close to the Equator are the hottest in the world.

Polar the Arctic and Antarctic have the coldest climates.

Temperate regions between the Poles and the Tropics usually have warm, dry summers and mild winters.

Land and sea

Coasts have a maritime climate. Sea temperature does not change much during the year so summers are cool but winters mild. Land far from the sea heats up and cools down more quickly so summers are hotter but winters colder. This is a continental climate.

DID YOU KNOW?

Temperate climates are thought to be the most pleasant to live in as they do not usually have extremes of hot or cold. Only 7% of the Earth's land surface has a temperate climate, yet nearly half the world's population lives in these areas.

City climates

In many places with a temperate climate the west end of a city is more fashionable than the east. This is because the wind usually blows from the west bringing fresh air to the west end and carrying smoke and pollution to the eastern side.

Extreme climates

Hottest and driest

Deserts are the hottest and driest places on Earth. In some deserts rain never falls. During the day it can be hot enough to fry an egg on the sand and at night cold enough for water to freeze.

Coldest

The Antarctic is the coldest and windiest place in the world with temperatures falling well below −50°C (−60°F). Even in midsummer, temperatures stay below freezing point.

Wettest

Near the Equator much of the land is covered in dense rain forest. The temperature is about 27°C (80°F) all year round. Heavy rain falls here every day.

Seasons

The seasons are caused by the Earth moving around the Sun and tilting at an angle to the Sun. They change as each half of the Earth leans towards or away from the Sun. When it is summer in the northern hemisphere it is winter in the south.

Most pleasant climate

Quito in Equador has earned the name 'Land of eternal spring' because of its climate. Temperatures never fall below 8°C (46°F) at night and reach 22°C (72°F) in the day. Every month about 100 mm (4 in) of refreshing rain falls.

Mountain sides

Mountains can affect the climate far away from them by diverting winds and rain. The sheltered (leeward) side of a mountain has dry weather because the air releases its rain as it rises up over the other (windward) side and cools.

Tropical season

Summer and winter are unknown in places near the Equator as the Equator never tilts away from the Sun. Some places have dry seasons and wet or monsoon seasons, others just hot and wet.

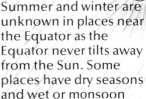

119

Special effects

Rainbows

If sunlight shines through drops of water it breaks up into its 7 main colours – red, orange, yellow, green, blue, indigo and violet. When sunlight hits raindrops or water spray a rainbow appears. To see a rainbow you must have your back to the Sun. From the ground you only see part of a full circle of colours.

Long bow

Rainbows usually only last for a few minutes. But a rainbow seen in Wales on 14 August 1979 was said to have lasted for three hours.

DID YOU KNOW?

Sometimes double rainbows can form. In a single bow red is always at the top and violet at the bottom. In the second fainter bow the colours are always the other way round.

St Elmo's fire

'St Elmo's fire' is a type of lightning which clings to ships' masts and the wing tips of aircraft. It is bluish-green or white and was named after a 4th century Italian bishop, Elmo, the patron saint of fire. Sailors prayed to him for protection at sea and took 'St Elmo's fire' to be a sign of good luck whenever it appeared.

Rings round the Sun

Whitish haloes round the Sun or Moon appear when light is bent by ice crystals in clouds high up in the atmosphere. Haloes are thought to be signs that rain is on its way and this is often

true. The Zuni Indians of North America believed that when the Sun was 'in his tepee' (that is, inside a halo) rain was likely to follow shortly afterwards.

Diamond dust

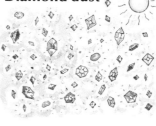

In very cold climates when temperatures drop to below −30°C (−22°F) water droplets in fog may freeze and the air fills with ice crystals. These fall slowly to the ground sparkling in the sunshine and are called ice fog or 'diamond dust'. It is dangerous if breathed in.

Mirages

Mirages are optical illusions. Light is bent as if passes through layers of air with different densities so distant objects look distorted.

Mirages are often seen over hot deserts or roads where a layer of heavy cold air lies over a layer of light warm air. Water may seem to appear on roads but this is really only the light from the sky reflected as if in a mirror. A similar reflection causes oases to appear in the desert.

Fata Morgana

One of the most beautiful mirages is the Fata Morgana, named after a fairy in a story. The mirage appears in the Strait of Messina, Italy as a town in the sky. Then a second town appears piled on top of the first, then a third. Each has splendid palaces and tall towers. People dressed in white seem to walk through the streets. No-one is sure what the mirage reflects but it may be one of the small fishing villages on the coast.

Amazing But True

Some fabulous animals were seen in the Gobi Desert by an American explorer, Roy Chapman Andrews. They looked like giant swans wading in a lake on legs 4½ m (15 ft) long. As Andrews went nearer, the water disappeared and the creatures changed shape. The giant swans were really antelopes grazing on the grass.

Red skies

At sunrise and sunset the sky is often a rich orange-red colour. This is because the short blue light waves in sunlight are scattered by dust in the air and only the longer red waves can get through. The colour of the sky is thought to show what the weather will be like. A red sky at night is said to be a sign of a fine day to come and a red sunrise a sign of bad weather.

Measuring the weather

Weather watching

There are about 10,000 weather stations all over the world in cities, at airports and on weather ships. Working together they watch the weather very closely. Every few hours they measure

humidity, wind speed and direction, pressure and temperature and check rain gauges. All this information is translated into an international code and sent round the world for forecasters to use.

Eureka

The Eureka weather station in Canada is the most remote in the world. It is 960 km (600 miles) from the North Pole – further north than any Eskimos live. Built in 1947, it has many luxuries including a greenhouse where staff grow plants during the 5 months when there is constant daylight.

Radiosonde

The weather high up in the atmosphere affects the weather on Earth. To measure it, balloons are sent up carrying instruments which radio information back to the ground. The balloons reach heights of 35-40 km (20-25 miles) and then burst. Small parachutes carry the instruments safely back to the ground.

Satellites

Satellites show weather patterns which cannot be seen from the ground. There are two types of weather satellites. Polar orbitting

satellites circle the Earth while geo-stationary satellites stay in a fixed place 35,000 km (22,000 miles) above the Equator. Cameras on board send back photographs of clouds.

Weather firsts

The first weather satellite was *Tiros I*, launched on 1 April 1960. It circled the Earth every two hours at heights of 700-1500 km (420-900 miles) and sent back pictures of cloud and snow cover.

Radar

Using radar, weathermen can see if rain is on the way. Each radar covers an area of about 200 km (124 miles) and picks up echo signals of the rain. On the radar screen the white patches are rain.

Storm tracking

In the USA radar is used to follow storms minute by minute so that tornado warnings can be given. In 1985 the Wimbledon tennis championships were saved by radar which saw a terrible storm coming. The groundstaff were warned in time to cover the courts.

Instruments for measuring weather

Weather	Instrument		Units
Atmospheric pressure	Barometer		Millibars
Temperature	Thermometer		°C/°F
Rainfall	Rain gauge		mm
Sunshine	Campbell Stokes recorder		Hours
Wind speed	Anemometer		Kph
Wind direction	Wind vane/ wind sock		NSEW
Humidity	Wet bulb thermometer		°C/°F

Cloud cover

The amount of cloud covering the sky is measured in eighths (oktas) from 1 to 8 oktas. 0 oktas means the sky is clear, 8 means it is completely covered. The height of a cloud is measured by how far its base is above sea level.

To measure sunshine, weathermen use a Campbell Stokes sunshine recorder. This is a glass ball which concentrates sunshine on to a thick piece of card. The sunshine burns a mark on the card which shows the number of hours of sunshine in the day.

Anemometer

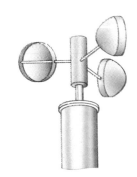

Anemometers measure wind speed. The most common type looks like a toy windmill. Three cups are fixed to a central shaft and the stronger the wind blows the faster they spin round. The wind speed in kph (mph) is shown on a dial, just like a car's speedometer.

Amazing But True

Human hair can be used to measure humidity. Hair expands in moist air and shrinks as it dries out. The change in length and in humidity can be measured using a hair hygrometer.

123

Forecasting the weather

Sign language

People were predicting the weather long before forecasts appeared on T.V. or in newspapers. They looked for 'signs' in the way plants and animals behave. When the pressure drops – a sign of bad weather – sheeps' wool uncurls and ants move to higher ground. Pine cones open when rain is about.

Weather maps

A forecaster is like a detective gathering information and clues. Detailed information about the weather at a certain time of the day is collected and plotted on a map, called a synoptic chart. From this the forecaster, using a computer, can work out very accurately what the next day's weather should be like.

Amazing But True

Animals can indicate the weather, often very accurately. The Germans used to keep frogs as live barometers because they croak when the pressure drops.

Isobars

Isobars are lines drawn on a synoptic chart joining together areas of equal pressure. The further apart they are, the lighter the wind. When they are close together the pressure is usually low and the wind is strong.

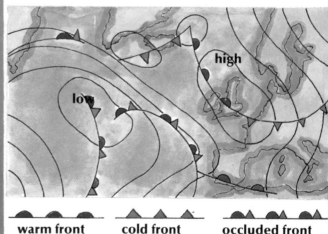

high

low

warm front   **cold front**   **occluded front**

Early warning

As long ago as the 5th century BC the Greeks sent out weather forecasts to their sailors. In the 4th century BC calendars of weather facts and forecasts called 'peg' calendars were put up on important buildings in many Greek cities and were very popular.

DID YOU KNOW?

The more observations there are the more accurate the forecasts will be. Ideally scientists would need frequent reports for every 15 cm^2 (2.3 in^2) of the Earth's surface. This means a report for each piece of the Earth just big enough to stand on.

Forecast factory

An English man, L. R. Richardson, was one of the first people to try to forecast the weather using mathematical equations. He worked out though that he would need a staff of 64,000 to do all the sums quickly enough.

Record forecasts

The U.S. Weather Service makes about 2 million forecasts a year. It also sends out storm and flood warnings and nearly 750,000 forecasts for aircraft. It claims that its one day forecasts are accurate more than three quarters of the time.

Computer age

Because computers can do difficult sums very quickly they have made forecasting much more accurate. The two largest computers are at the weather centres in Washington, USA and Bracknell, UK. The Bracknell computer can handle 400 million calculations a second.

False alarm

In 1185 an astronomer, Johannes of Toledo, predicted that the following year a terrible wind would bring famine and destruction to Europe. People were so frightened that some built new homes underground. But nothing happened!

Who uses forecasts?

Forecasts are used everyday to help us decide what to wear and where to go. They are vital to pilots, sailors and farmers who need to know exactly what weather to expect. If cold weather is on the way more electricity is made and chemists stock more cold cures. Dairies make more ice-cream if hot weather is expected.

Two types of forecast

There are two types of forecast – short and long range. Computers help forecasters produce short range charts for up to a week ahead. Long range forecasting is less accurate and is often done by looking at past weather records. In India forecasts have been made of the next year's monsoon so that famine can be prevented if the rain fails as often happens.

125

Weather wear and tear

Wear and tear

Rain, wind and frost are always wearing away the Earth's surface. This is called weathering. Rain collects in cracks in the rocks. If it freezes it expands and cracks the rocks apart with a force of 90 kg (200 lb) per 6 sq cm (1 sq in) to form crevices. The wind carries away small pieces of rock chipped off when crevices form.

DID YOU KNOW?

Weathering is very slow. The height of some mountains is lowered by about 8.6 cm (3½ in) every 1,000 years. At this rate a mountain only as tall as the Eiffel Tower would take over 3 million years to wear right down.

Wind on sand

Sand blown by the wind helps to shape deserts. Wind blowing constantly from one direction piles the sand up into sanddunes. As more sand is blown across the top of a dune and trickles down the other side, the dune rolls forward like a wave. Small dunes can move more than 15 m (50 ft) a year and can bury whole villages as they pass. The two main types of dune are barchan and seif. The much larger seif dunes can be up to 400 km (250 miles) long.

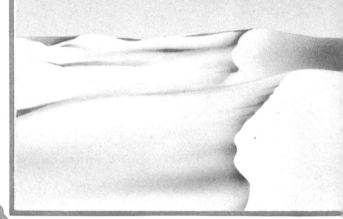

Highest dunes

The highest measured sanddunes in the world are in the Sahara Desert. They can reach a height of 430 m (1410 ft) – nearly as high as the Sears Tower in Chicago, USA.

Sand saucers

Huge 'saucers' have been scooped out of the Sahara Desert by windblown sand. The Qattara Depression in Egypt is a huge hollow area below sea-level which is almost the size of Wales.

Fairy forest

Trees growing very high up on mountain sides have to grow close to the ground for protection from the strong cold wind. They are forced to grow sideways and become twisted. These are called krummholz trees or elfin wood. Some fir and pine trees grow so close to the ground that you can step right over them.

Weather and crops

Temperature and rainfall are the most important influences on growing crops. There is an ideal climate for every crop and farmers have to consider their local climate before choosing which are the best crops to grow.

Weather beaters

Scientists are now at work creating crops which can survive in harsh climates. These include potatoes and sugar beet which can live through droughts and barley which is not killed by frost.

Irrigation

In places with little rainfall, water is stored in reservoirs and tanks and used for crops and for drinking. In the USA irrigation accounts for nearly half of the water used. The world's longest irrigation canal is in the USSR. It is 850 km (528 miles) long, over twice as long as Britain's River Thames.

Ice slice

Glaciers are huge rivers of ice which move slowly down mountain slopes. In the last Ice Age rocks in the underside of the ice scraped and tore away deep valleys like the Norwegian fjords.

Crops and climate

Crop	Ideal climate
oranges	warm and sunny
rice	warm and wet
maize	warm and wet in summer
oats	quite cool and wet
potatoes	cool and wet

Living with the weather

Weather wear

People wear clothes suited to the climate they live in. In hot places like the Middle East they wear long, loose robes specially folded so that cool air is trapped inside. In the desert people wear turbans and veils to protect their heads and faces from the Sun and sand. Fur is worn in cold places because it is very good at keeping out the cold.

DID YOU KNOW?

The hot, dry Föhn and Scirocco winds are said to damage the health. During the Föhn the accident, crime and suicide rates in Germany rise. The Scirocco is said to cause madness.

Aches and pains

There may be some truth in the saying that people can feel the weather in their bones. Some people find that they have aches and pains when the air is humid. Others get headaches before a thunderstorm.

Body guard

The body protects itself from too much heat or cold by perspiring or shivering. Shivering is caused by the muscles twitching and giving off heat. Perspiration is the body's own air-conditioner. It evaporates off the skin and cools it down.

Lifestyles

Weather affects the way people live. In the desert people such as the Bedouins of the Sahara live a nomadic life. They move from place to place in search of water and fodder for their animals. They live in tents to make moving house easier.

Windcatchers

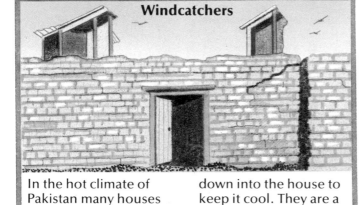

In the hot climate of Pakistan many houses have windcatchers on their roofs. These trap the wind and direct it down into the house to keep it cool. They are a simple but very effective system of natural air-conditioning.

Sleepy head

Animals react to changes in the weather. Some hibernate in winter when food is short. Their pulse and breathing rates slow down to save energy. A hibernating hedgehog only breathes once every 6 seconds – 200 times slower than its normal breathing rate.

Water frog

The water-holding frog which lives in the Central Australian Desert only has a drink every five to six years. This is how often rain falls. Then the frog comes to the surface and absorbs about half its own weight in water so it looks like a small balloon. This supply keeps the frog alive during the droughts.

Amazing But True

The higher you go the thinner the air and the harder it is to breathe. But people have been able to adapt. Andean Indians, living in mountain villages at about 5,200 m (17,000 ft) have larger lungs and hearts than normal so they can breathe properly even at this great height.

Skin shield

People who live in hot climates have darker skins to protect them from the Sun. Their skin contains a lot of melanin, a brown pigment which acts as a shield against the Sun's harmful ultra-violet rays. Fair-skinned people tend to get sunburnt easily as they are not so well protected.

Ice house

Eskimos used to build their homes out of snow to make use of the Arctic climate they live in. Igloos are quick to build. Blocks of snow are made into a circular base then more circles are added on top, each smaller than the last. An air hole is left at the top and an entrance tunnel built. Snow is such a good insulator that it keeps the inside of the igloo warm and snug though the outside walls stay frozen.

Changing the weather

Warmly wrapped

Most scientists think that the Earth is getting warmer. Burning coal, oil and forests increases the amount of the gas carbon dioxide in the atmosphere. This acts like a giant blanket round the Earth keeping in warmth which would otherwise escape. If the amount of carbon dioxide in the air was doubled the Earth's temperature would rise by 2°C (4°F).

Fog clearing

Fog can cause accidents and delays at airports. Many airports today have huge pipes along the sides of the runways. Fuel is pumped into them and burned. This raises the air temperature so that the fog evaporates and planes can take off and land safely.

Acid rain

The rain which falls on parts of Europe and North America can be more acid than lemon juice. Acid rain falls when gases and chemicals from factories dissolve in water in the air to form weak acids. Pollution carried by the wind can fall as acid rain hundreds of kilometers away and destroy forests, crops and life in lakes and rivers.

Amazing But True

Some scientists think that the Earth is getting colder as more pollution in the air blocks out more of the Sun's heat. They have thought of some unusual ways to prevent a new Ice Age.

One of their ideas is to spread vast black plastic sheets or layers of soot over the Polar ice caps. The black surface would absorb heat from the Sun and cause the ice to melt.

If the ice melted

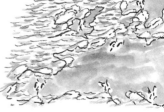

If the Earth became even a few degrees warmer the ice at the Poles would melt and the sea-level rise by about 60 m (200 ft). Coastal cities like New York, Bombay, London and Sydney would be drowned.

Traffic trouble

In many big cities the air is being polluted by exhaust fumes from cars, lorries and buses. Smog, a mixture of smoke and fog, forms when these fumes react with sunlight. In Los Angeles, USA and Tokyo, Japan thick smog is a serious problem. It can damage people's health and destroy stone buildings and crops.

Pea-soupers

Until the 1960s London had terrible, thick smogs called pea-soupers which were coloured green by smoke from factories and coal fires. The worst pea-souper was in December 1952. Some 4,000 people died from bronchitis and pneumonia.

Making rain

To make artificial rain, crystals of silver iodide are shot into clouds from aircraft. Water in the cloud freezes round them and falls as rain or snow. No-one knows how well this works.

Aerosol cans used for hairsprays and paints may be harmful. They contain gases called freons which, some scientists think, destroy the gas ozone 24 km (15 miles) up in the atmosphere. Without the ozone layer we would die because it protects us from the Sun's harmful ultra-violet rays.

Rain forests

Every three seconds a piece of South American rain forest the size of a football pitch is cut down. This may lead to changes in rainfall and temperature around the world. Trees 'breathe out' water vapour which is turned into rain in the water cycle. Destroying the forests means that less water vapour is made and less rain falls. Burning the trees increases the amount of carbon dioxide in the air and may be making the Earth warmer.

Weather of the past

Ice Ages

The Earth's climate changes very slowly over the centuries. It is made up of warm periods (interglacials) and cold periods (glacials) or Ice Ages. We live in an interglacial which began about 10,000 years ago. The last glacial was 19,000 years ago when a third of the Earth lay under an ice sheet some 244 m (800 ft) thick.

How Ice Ages happen

Ice Ages are caused by changes in the Earth's orbit round the Sun. Even the tiniest difference in the Earth's path can alter the amount of heat the Earth receives from the Sun and plunge it into a freezing Ice Age.

DID YOU KNOW?

A change in climate may have been the reason for dinosaurs becoming extinct about 65 million years ago. At this time, some people believe, a meteor struck the Earth causing a dust cloud to block out the Sun's heat and the Earth became very cold. Dinosaurs were probably cold-blooded and so froze to death.

Ice cores

One way of finding out about past climates is by drilling holes in glaciers and pulling out long cores of ice. Distinct layers can be seen in the ice. The darker the ice the colder the climate was. An ice core 366 m (1200 ft) long can tell us about the weather of the past 1400 years.

Climate clues

Scientists find clues about the Earth's past in fossils, soils and trees. Every year a tree grows a new ring. If the ring is wide the weather was

moist and warm, if narrow then it was dry and cold. Tree ring dating gives the most reliable picture of the weather of the past. Bristlecone pines in the USA give the longest record. Some are over 4,000 years old.

Viking voyages

From AD 1000-1200 the world's weather became warmer. The Arctic ice melted and the Vikings were able to sail north from Scandinavia to Greenland which was about 1-4°C (2-7°F) warmer than today. They also sailed across the Atlantic to North America. Today's storms and icebergs would make this route very dangerous for the light, wooden Viking boats.

Frost fairs

During the Little Ice Age the River Thames in London froze over in winter and fairs were held on the ice. The first was in 1607. Tents were set up and there were swings, foodstalls and sideshows. In the winter of 1683 the ice was 26 cm (10 in) thick. The last frost fair was in 1813. It only lasted a few days but the ice was strong enough for an elephant to walk on.

Little Ice Age

From about AD 1400 the Earth's climate became much colder and the 'Little Ice Age' began. In the winter of 1431 every river in Germany froze over. The cold weather lasted until about 1850. Arctic pack ice stretched towards the Equator and the temperature was about 2-4°C (4-7°F) lower than today.

Saharan seasons

About 450 million years ago the Sahara Desert was covered in ice. But from about 4000-2000 BC it was covered in grass and trees. Cave paintings from Tassili, Algeria which date from that time, show people hunting and lions, buffalo and elephants roaming wild.

Amazing But True

London, England was a very different place 50 million years ago. It had a hot, humid climate and was covered in marshy swamps and tropical jungle where hippos, turtles and crocodiles lived.

Weather gods

Weather power

Good harvests depend on good weather. Early farmers, such as the Sumerians, who lived 7,000 years ago, thought gods ruled the weather. These gods were worshipped with prayers and sacrifices. People today still pray for fine weather and for a good harvest.

Blood-thirsty Sun

The Aztecs believed that the Sun god, Huitzilopochti, was a warrior who fought against the power of night so that the Sun could be reborn every morning. He had to be kept strong and people were sacrificed to provide him with human hearts and blood which were thought to be his favourite food.

DID YOU KNOW?

Some early primitive people thought that evil spirits lived in the clouds who sent down hail to destroy their crops. They used to shoot arrows into the clouds to frighten the spirits away.

Wind worship

The Ancient Greeks gave the winds names and characters. The Tower of the Winds in Athens, built in 100 BC, shows one of the eight main winds on each wall. Each is dressed for the weather it brings.

Boreas (North)
Notos (South)
Zephyros (West)
Apeliotes (East)
Kaikas (North East)
Euros (South East)
Lips (South West)
Skiros (North West)

Re and Nut

Like the Aztecs, the Ancient Egyptians believed that the gods ruled everything in nature. Their most important god was Re, the Sun god whose mother, Nut, was the sky goddess. Nut was held up by the god of air who stood over the god of Earth.

Sun kings

Many people have worshipped the Sun as the source of life itself. The Ancient Egyptians even believed that their Pharoah was the son of the Sun god, and in Japan the Emperor was thought to be a direct descendant of the Sun goddess.

Thunderous Thor

Thor was the Norse god of thunder. He was thought to be very strong and have wild red hair and a beard. Thor raced across the sky in a chariot pulled by two giant goats and brewed up storms by blowing through his beard. He lived in a great hall called Bilskirnir which means lightning.

Dragon breath

The Chinese believed that dragons formed clouds with their breath and brought rain. The rain fell when the dragons walked over the clouds and storms raged when they fought with each other.

Hot dog days

The Romans called the hottest days of summer 'dog days'. They linked the weather with the stars, and at this time Sirius, the Dog star, was the brightest in the sky.

Chinese calendar

In the 3rd century BC the Chinese divided the year into 24 festivals connected with the weather. Each season had six festivals telling people what weather to expect so that they could sow and harvest their crops at the right times.

Rainbow god

The Kabi people from Queensland in Australia worship a god called Dhakhan who is half fish and half snake. Dhakhan lives in deep water holes in the ground. He appears as a rainbow in the sky when he moves from one hole to the next.

Dancing in the rain

The Hopi Indians of North America perform special rain dances like the buffalo and snake dances. As they dance they pray to the gods to send them rain.

Water everywhere

There are many stories about a great flood which nearly destroyed mankind. The Bible tells of Noah and the Ark. In the Babylonian poem 'Gilgamesh' a violent storm drowns the Earth. In the Greek myth Zeus sends the flood to punish people for being so wicked.

Freaks and disasters

Iced turtle

During a severe hailstorm on 11 May 1894 near Vicksburg, USA a gophar turtle the size of a brick fell with the hail. It had been bounced up and down in a thunder cloud and coated in layer after layer of ice.

Worst weather disasters

Disaster	Location	Date	Deaths
Drought/famine	Bengal, India	1943-4	1,500,000
Flood	Henan, China	1939	1,000,000
Hurricane	Bangladesh	1970	1,000,000
Smog	London, UK	1952	2,850
Tornado	Missouri, USA	1925	800
Hail	Moredabad, India	1888	246
Lightning	Umtali, Zimbabwe	1975	21

Desert snow

Snow fell in the Kalahari Desert in Africa on 1 September 1981 – the first time in living memory. Temperatures dropped as low as −5°C (23°F).

Food from the sky

The sky over Turkey rained down food in August 1890. A type of edible lichen fell with the rain which the local people collected and made into bread.

Hot and cold

On 22 January 1943 a freezing cold winter's day in South Dakota, USA was transformed into a balmy spring one. At precisely 7.30 in the morning the temperature rose an amazing 27°C (49°F) in just two minutes.

Amazing But True

On 14 October 1755 rain the colour of blood fell in Locarno, Switzerland and red snow fell over the Alps. This odd colouring was caused by dust from the Sahara Desert in North Africa which had been carried over 3,000 km (1,850 miles) by the wind.

Leg strike

Lightning can fuse or melt metal together. On 10 August 1975 a cricket umpire in England was struck by lightning. He was not hurt but the knee joint in his false metal leg was welded quite solid!

Out of the blue

Thirty workers picking peppers in Arizona, USA were knocked down by a flash of lightning which appeared out of a clear sky. Three died and many were injured.

About turn

A tornado in the USA picked up a railway engine, turned it round in mid-air and put it down again on a parallel track running in the other direction.

Watery walkways

The captain of a ship bound for Uruguay in 1929 reported seeing the unique sight of two large clouds connected by two waterspouts. Waterspouts have often been mistaken for sea monsters.

Pennies from heaven

In June 1940 a shower of silver coins fell in Gorky, USSR. A tornado uncovered an old treasure chest, lifted it into the air and dropped some 1,000 coins on a nearby village.

DID YOU KNOW?

There have been many reports of showers of fish and frogs. On 16 June 1939 a shower of tiny frogs fell at Trowbridge in England. Strong winds had sucked the frogs up from ponds and streams nearby and they then fell with the rain.

Wild weather

Drought **Wet**
Ice **Heatwave**

In 1972 many places had unusual weather. On the Arctic coast the temperature reached 32°C (90°F) for several days. In the USSR a heatwave caused disastrous forest fires and in India the monsoon rains failed. In Peru and the Philippines, however, there was very heavy rain and flooding.

Television weather maps

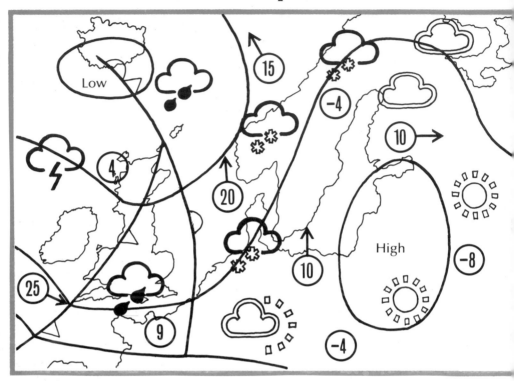

Fronts

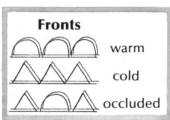	warm
	cold
	occluded

Some weather symbols

(12) Temperature (°C)

Sunshine

Fair weather cloud

Dull weather cloud

Sunny intervals

Rain

Rain with sunny intervals

Snow

Thunderstorm

(16) → Wind speed and direction

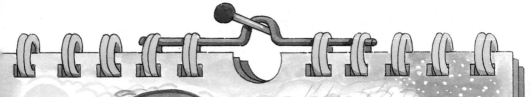

Weather calendar

1st century AD Hero of Alexandria (Ancient Greece) was probably the first to discover that air had weight.

1607 The first Frost Fair was held on the frozen river Thames in London with tents, sideshows and foodstalls.

1611 Johann Kepler (Germany) was the first person to describe the six-sided shape of snowflakes.

1643 Evangelista Torricelli (Italy) invented the first barometer for measuring air pressure.

1654 Grand Duke Ferdinand of Tuscany invented the first sealed thermometer for measuring temperature.

1718 Gabriel Daniel Fahrenheit (Germany) devised the Fahrenheit scale (°F) for measuring temperature.

1722 Reverend Horsley (Britain) invented the first modern rain gauge. The earliest mention of a rain gauge is in Indian writings from 400 BC.

1742 Anders Celsius (Sweden) devised the Celsius or Centigrade scale (°C) for measuring temperature.

1752 Benjamin Franklin (USA) invented the lightning conductor for use on high buildings.

1783 Horace-Bénédict de Saussure (Switzerland) made the first hair hygrometer for measuring humidity.

1802 Luke Howard (Britain) named the three families of clouds – cirrus, cumulus and stratus.

1805 Admiral Sir Francis Beaufort (Britain) devised the Beaufort Scale for measuring wind speed at sea.

1843 Lucien Vidie (France) made the first aneroid ('non-liquid') barometer for measuring air pressure.

1846 John Robinson (Britain) invented the cup anemometer for measuring wind speed and direction.

1851 The first published weather maps were sold to the public at the Great Exhibition in London.

1856 The first national storm warning system was started in France after storms destroyed ships during the Crimean War.

c.1887 Clement Wragge (Australia) was the first person to give hurricanes names. They are still named today.

1930 Pierre Molchanov (USSR) launched a radiosonde for measuring weather in the upper atmosphere.

c.1945 John von Neumann (USA) built an electronic computer known as *Maniac*. It was the first to be used for weather forecasting.

1960 The first weather satellite, *Tiros I*, was launched by the USA.

Weather record breakers

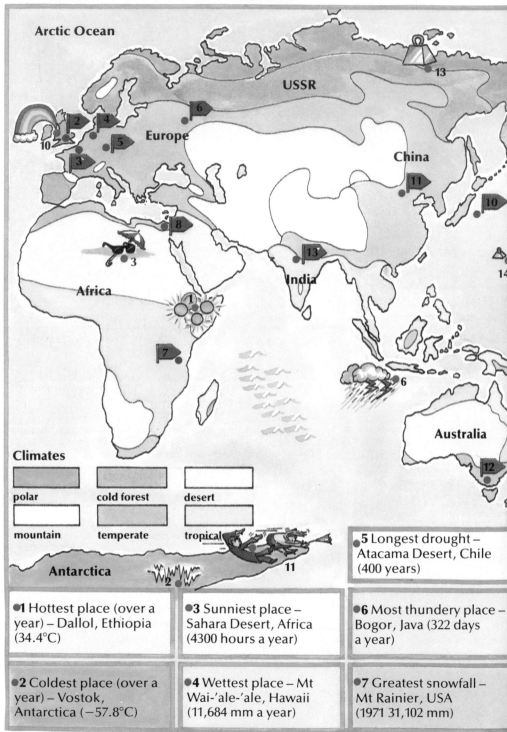

Arctic Ocean

USSR

Europe

China

Africa

India

Australia

Antarctica

Climates

polar

cold forest

desert

mountain

temperate

tropical

●1 Hottest place (over a year) – Dallol, Ethiopia (34.4°C)

●2 Coldest place (over a year) – Vostok, Antarctica (−57.8°C)

●3 Sunniest place – Sahara Desert, Africa (4300 hours a year)

●4 Wettest place – Mt Wai-'ale-'ale, Hawaii (11,684 mm a year)

●5 Longest drought – Atacama Desert, Chile (400 years)

●6 Most thundery place – Bogor, Java (322 days a year)

●7 Greatest snowfall – Mt Rainier, USA (1971 31,102 mm)

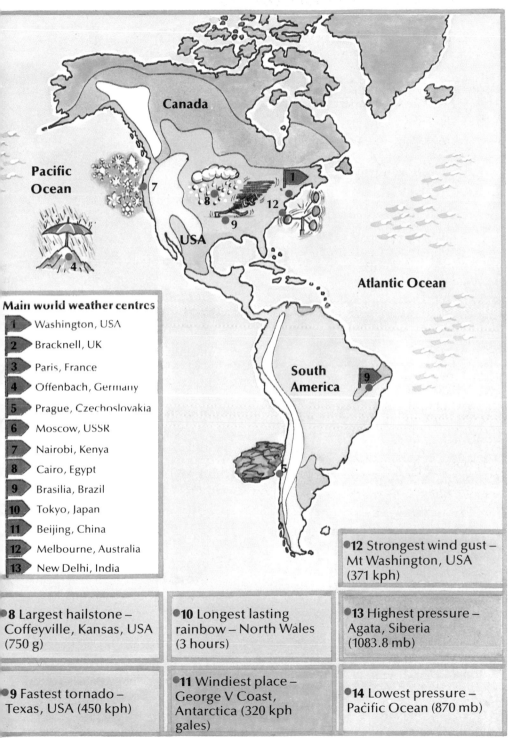

Main world weather centres

1 Washington, USA
2 Bracknell, UK
3 Paris, France
4 Offenbach, Germany
5 Prague, Czechoslovakia
6 Moscow, USSR
7 Nairobi, Kenya
8 Cairo, Egypt
9 Brasilia, Brazil
10 Tokyo, Japan
11 Beijing, China
12 Melbourne, Australia
13 New Delhi, India

Canada

Pacific Ocean

USA

Atlantic Ocean

South America

12 Strongest wind gust – Mt Washington, USA (371 kph)

8 Largest hailstone – Coffeyville, Kansas, USA (750 g)

10 Longest lasting rainbow – North Wales (3 hours)

13 Highest pressure – Agata, Siberia (1083.8 mb)

9 Fastest tornado – Texas, USA (450 kph)

11 Windiest place – George V Coast, Antarctica (320 kph gales)

14 Lowest pressure – Pacific Ocean (870 mb)

141

Glossary

Air mass Huge mass of cold or warm air which moves around the world. Can be dry or moist.

Air pressure The weight of the atmosphere pressing down on the Earth's surface.

Anemometer Instrument used to measure wind speed.

Atmosphere The blanket of air around the Earth.

Barometer Instrument used to measure air pressure.

Celsius Degrees (°C) used for measuring temperature. Also called Centigrade.

Climate The general weather of a place over a long period of time.

Cloud A mass of tiny water droplets or ice crystals.

Cold front Boundary between two different air masses where cold air pushes warm air away. Usually means colder weather.

Condensation When water vapour cools and turns into liquid water.

Coriolis effect The bending of the winds caused by the Earth spinning on its axis.

Dew point The temperature at which the air cannot hold any more water vapour and condensation begins.

Evaporation When liquid water is heated and turns into water vapour.

Fahrenheit Degrees (°F) used for measuring temperature.

High (anticyclone) Area of high pressure. Brings dry weather.

Humidity The amount of moisture in the form of water vapour there is in the air.

Hygrometer Instrument used to measure humidity.

Isobars Lines drawn on a weather map, joining places of equal pressure.

Jet stream Strong wind 5-10 km up in the atmosphere.

Low (depression) Area of low pressure. Often brings wet weather.

Meteorology The scientific study of the atmosphere and weather.

Meteorologists Scientists who study the atmosphere and weather.

Millibar Unit (mb) used to measure air pressure.

Occluded front Combination of warm and cold fronts as cold air overtakes warm front.

Precipitation Water which falls from a cloud as rain, snow or hail.

Radiosonde Instruments attached to a balloon for measuring the weather in the upper atmosphere.

Synoptic chart Weather map using isobars to show highs, lows and fronts.

Thermometer Instrument used to measure temperature.

Troposphere The lowest level of the atmosphere, directly above the ground, where weather happens.

Warm front Boundary between two different air masses where warm air pushes cold air away to bring warmer weather.

Water vapour Water in gas form which is in the atmosphere and helps make the weather.

Weather The state of the air at a certain time and place. Temperature, humidity, wind, cloud and precipitation.

Index

SPACE FACTS

Struan Reid

CONTENTS

Illustrated by Tony Gibson

**Additional illustrations by
Martin Newton**

Designed by Teresa Foster

Additional designs by Tony Gibson

Consultant: Sue Becklake

What's it all about?

Astronomy

What is a star? How big is the Universe? Where did the Sun and Earth come from? These are some of the questions that people have been asking for thousands of years. Astronomy is the science that tries to answer these questions and the job of the astronomer is to try and understand the Universe.

Delayed timing

Light from the Sun takes over eight minutes to reach us, travelling a distance of 150 million km (93 million miles). It takes eleven hours to reach the furthest planet in our Solar System, which is Pluto.

A special measurement

The Universe is so enormous that astronomers use a special measurement known as a light year. This is the distance light travels in one year, or 9.5 million, million km (about 6 million, million miles). Light travels at a speed of 300,000 km (186,000 miles) per second.

One of the family

The Earth on which we live is one of a family of nine planets travelling round the Sun. Together they are known as the Solar System. The Sun itself is one very ordinary star in our galaxy, the Milky Way, which contains about 100,000 million stars altogether.

Sun Mercury Venus Earth Mars Jupiter Saturn Uranus Neptune Pluto

One among many

Our own galaxy measures about 950,000 million, million km across. It is only one among millions of other galaxies. All the galaxies and the space around them make up the Universe.

As far as we can see

THE END OF THE UNIVERSE?

The furthest distance astronomers can see into the Universe is about 15,000 million light years, although this is not necessarily the edge of the Universe. It might not even have a boundary.

Amazing But True

If it was possible to travel in a spacecraft at the speed of light, you could go round the Earth seven times in just one second.

The light reaching us now from our nearest star set off over four years ago. At present rocket speeds it would probably take thousands of years to get to the nearest star and back.

The scale of the Universe

The distances in the Universe are so great that it is difficult to imagine them. If the Sun was the size of a ball 1.8 m (6 ft) across, then Pluto, the most distant planet in our Solar System, would be the size of a pea 7.6 km (4.7 miles) away. But our nearest star would be about 52,000 km (32,313 miles) away.

We've only just begun

The exploration of space by satellites and spacecraft is helping scientists learn more about our neighbouring worlds in the Solar System and about the Universe as a whole. But so far we have only been able to explore two other planets in our Solar System with unmanned spacecraft.

Future meetings

In the future we may be able to travel as far as the stars and land on their planets. Some stars may have planets on which other beings live whom we may be able to visit or contact by radio.

Going up Our Universe at different heights

A 1 km: low altitude.

B 10,000 km: high.

C 1 million km: Earth-Moon system.

D 10 million, million km: 1 light year.

E 100,000 light years: Milky Way galaxy.

F 15,000 million light years: limits of the observable Universe.

Now read on

This book tells you about some of the discoveries that have been made and the possible plans for the future, some of which may happen in your own lifetime.

The Solar System

The Sun's family

All the planets surrounding the Sun are members of the Sun's family, known as the Solar System. The Sun lies at the centre of the family and orbiting (circling) round it are the planets and their moons and also the asteroids.

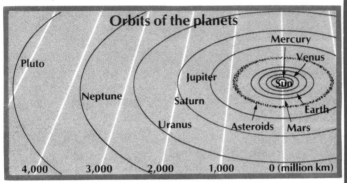

Orbits of the planets

Pluto
Neptune
Uranus
Jupiter
Saturn
Asteroids
Mercury
Venus
Sun
Earth
Mars

4,000   3,000   2,000   1,000   0 (million km)

The Sun's diameter of 1,392,000 km (865,000 miles) is about 109 times that of Earth's and 10 times that of Jupiter's. If the Sun were represented by a beach ball with a 50 cm (20 in) diameter, Mars would be the size of a small pea about 55 m (180 ft) away and Jupiter would be the size of a golfball 280 m (919 ft) away.

Birth in a cloud

Many scientists think that the Solar System was formed from a cloud of gas and dust about 4,600 million years ago. The Sun formed in the centre while the planets grew from balls of gas round it.

Gas condenses

Sun born

Planets form

Solar System born

Merry-go-round

All the members of the Solar System move about other objects. The moons are circling their parent planets, the planets circle the Sun, while each spins about its axis at the same time. The Sun also spins and the whole Solar System is travelling round the galaxy it lies in.

Messenger of the gods

Named after the speedy messenger of the Roman gods, Mercury travels round the Sun at the fastest speed of all the planets, about 172,248 kph (107,030 mph).

The Sun gives off huge amounts of deadly radiation, but we are protected from the worst blasts by a magnetic cage called the magnetosphere that surrounds the Earth. Inside this cage, two doughnut-shaped belts trap the electric particles. These are called the Van Allen belts after their discoverer, James Van Allen.

Brightest and faintest

Viewed from Earth, by far the brightest of the planets visible to the naked eye is Venus. It is often called the "evening star". The faintest planet is Pluto. It can only be seen through a telescope.

Data

Planet	Rotational period (round axis)	Orbital period (round Sun)
Mercury	58.7 days	88 days
Venus	243 days	224.7 days
Earth	23.93 hrs	365.25 days
Mars	24.62 hrs	687 days
Jupiter	9.92 hrs	11.9 years
Saturn	10.23 hrs	29.5 years
Uranus	17 hrs	84 years
Neptune	18 hrs	165 years
Pluto	6.4 days	248 years

The unique planet

The Earth is a very special planet because it is the only place in the Solar System, and the only known place in the entire Universe, to support life. If it was closer to the Sun it would be too hot to support life and if it was further away it would be too cold.

Fast spinner

Jupiter is the fastest spinning planet in our Solar System. If you could stand on the equator of the planet, you would be travelling at a speed of 45,500 kph (28,273 mph), compared with the Earth's speed of 523 kph (325 mph).

The Sun

One among millions

The Sun is a star, one of 100,000 million stars in our galaxy, the Milky Way. Although it is a very ordinary star in the galaxy, it is very important in our Solar System; without it there would be no life on Earth.

Sizing up the Sun

If the Sun was the size of a large orange, the Earth would be the size of a tiny seed about 10 m (33 ft) away.

Great ball of fire

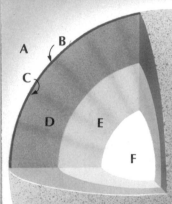

The Sun is mainly made up of the lightest gas, called hydrogen. It burns up 700 million tonnes of hydrogen every second in nuclear reactions at its centre. Scientists believe the Sun loses 4 million tonnes of gas every second, which is about the weight of one million elephants.

A Corona (outer part of the Sun's atmosphere) – 2 million°C.

B Chromosphere (9,600 km/6,000 miles deep) – 4,000°C to more than 50,000°C at the top.

C Photosphere (400 km/249 miles deep) – 6,000°C.

D Convective zone (where gases move round).

E Radiative zone.

F Solar interior – 15 million°C. Nuclear reactions take place here.

Amazing But True

One second of the energy given off by the Sun is 13 million times greater than the average amount of electricity used each year in the USA. All the Earth's oil, coal and wood supplies would fuel the Sun for only a few days.

A long car drive

The distance of the Sun from Earth is just under 150 million km (93 million miles). This distance is called an astronomical unit. If you drove a car at 88 kph (55 mph) from the Earth to the Sun it would take 193 years.

Dangerous heat

The temperature at the centre of the Sun reaches 15 million °C (27 million °F). If a pinhead was this hot, it would set light and destroy everything for 100 km (60 miles) around it.

Deadly breeze

The Sun gives off a stream of particles charged with electricity. This is called the solar wind and is estimated to blow more than twice as far as Pluto, the furthest planet in the Solar System.

Light shows

Glowing coloured lights, called aurorae, can sometimes be seen in the skies of the north and south poles. They happen when the electric particles from the Sun bump into the gases in the Earth's atmosphere and make them glow.

The Sun's beauty spots

Areas of gas that are cooler than the rest of the surface appear as dark patches on the Sun and are called sunspots. They only seem dark in comparison to the brilliant surrounding surface. Eight Earths can fit into the area of one sunspot.

Fiery fountains

Fountains of burning hydrogen and helium gas called solar prominences flare up in the Sun's chromosphere. The greatest solar prominence ever recorded reached a height of 402,000 km (250,000 miles), more than the distance from Earth to the Moon.

Why a battle ended

Eclipses of the Sun take place when the Sun, Moon and Earth are all lined up so that the Moon blocks out the sunlight. In 585BC an eclipse happened in the middle of a battle between the Lydians and Medes. The armies made peace.

The Moon

Data

Diameter at the equator: 3,476 km

Mass: 0.0123 (Earth = 1. It would take 81 Moons to equal the mass of the Earth.)

Surface gravity: 0.17 (Earth = 1)

Distance from Earth
furthest: 406,700 km
nearest: 356,400 km
average: 384,000 km

Rotational period round Earth: 27.3 Earth-days

Our nearest neighbour

The Moon is the closest neighbour to Earth. Its average distance from Earth is only 384,000 km (239,000 miles). A train travelling at 161 kph (100 mph) would take 99.5 days to cover the distance.

Phases of the Moon

From Earth, the Moon seems to change shape, from a sliver to a full Moon and back to a sliver again. This is because we see different amounts of the Moon's sunlit side as it moves round the Earth. The different shapes are called phases and the Moon goes through its phases in 29.5 days.

DID YOU KNOW?

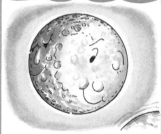

The Moon takes just over 27 days to travel round the Earth. It always keeps the same half facing the Earth. The far side of the Moon had never been seen until the USSR spacecraft Luna 3 took the first photographs of it in 1959.

Pockmarked surface

About 500,000 Moon craters can be seen through the most powerful telescopes. It would take someone about 400 hours to count all of them – and just those on the face that we can see.

A Scottish crater

The largest crater we can see on the Moon is called Bailly and covers an area of about 67,300 square km (26,000 square miles). If Bailly was brought down to Earth, Scotland could sit comfortably inside it.

Seas without water

The dark areas you can see on the Moon's surface are called "seas". There is no water there but millions of years ago they were covered by volcanic lava. Some are very big. The Ocean of Storms is larger than the Mediterranean.

As dry as dust

The Moon has no atmosphere and contains no water. Its soil is so dry that nothing will grow in it. But scientists have found that with air and water, plants can grow in Moon soil on Earth.

Dead quiet

The Moon is a completely silent place. Noises cannot be heard as there is no air to carry sound from one place to another.

Precious stones

The various Apollo astronauts who landed on the Moon brought back to Earth a total of 382 kg (842 lb) of Moon rocks and dust. Divided into the total cost of the Apollo space programme, the samples of Moon rock and dust cost around $67,000 per gram ($1,896,000 per ounce).

Staying the same

Unlike the Earth, which has been continuously worn away, the surface of the Moon has not been attacked by wind and water. The rocks brought back to Earth by astronauts had probably been lying in the same position on the surface of the Moon for 3,000 million years without moving a fraction.

Amazing But True

Footprints left on the Moon by the Apollo astronauts will probably be visible for at least 10 million years.

Moonquivers

There are earthquakes on the Moon known as moonquakes, but they are very weak compared to our earthquakes. About 3,000 occur each year, but all the moonquakes in one year would produce enough energy for just a small fireworks display.

Gravity and tides

The pull of gravity of the Earth on the Moon keeps the Moon circling round the Earth. But the Moon's gravity also pulls the water in the Earth's seas towards it, causing the Earth's tides. If the Moon was closer to Earth the pull of its gravity would be much stronger and the tides would flood the coastlines of the world.

Mercury, Venus and Mars

Data

Planet	Diameter at the equator	Mass	Orbital speed (round Sun)	Surface temperatures	Satellites
Mercury	4,878 km	0.055 (Earth=1)	47.9 km/sec	350°C	0
Venus	12,100 km	0.815	35.0 km/sec	480°C	0
Mars	6,780 km	0.107	24.1 km/sec	–23°C	2

The inner planets

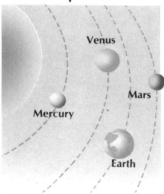

Mercury, Venus and Mars, along with the Earth, form a group of four rocky planets unlike the others. They are known as the inner planets because they are the nearest to the Sun.

Hotter than a desert

Mercury is the closest planet to the Sun. Because of this, it has scorching daytime temperatures of up to 350°C (662°F). This is over seven times hotter than the hottest temperature ever recorded on Earth – 57.7°C (136°F) at Azizia, Libya in 1922.

Freezer cold

The temperature on Mercury at night can plunge to –170°C (–274°F), because there is no blanket of atmosphere to trap the heat. This is more than seven times colder than the temperature inside the freezer compartment of a refrigerator.

DID YOU KNOW?

Mercury has a core of iron, slightly bigger than our Moon. At recent world production figures for iron, it would take about 6,500 million years to mine all the iron in Mercury's core.

Not really an atmosphere

Although Mercury is surrounded by a thin layer of helium gas, there is so little of it that the amount collected from a 6.4 km (4 mile) diameter sphere would be just enough to fill a child's small balloon.

Clouds of acid

Although Venus and Earth are about the same size, their atmospheres are completely different. Venus' atmosphere is made up mostly of carbon dioxide gas, which is poisonous, and contains sulphuric acid in its clouds.

Deep atmosphere diving

Venus' atmosphere is so thick that at the planet's surface the pressure is 90 times that on Earth. On Earth, the atmospheric pressure measures 1.03 kg cm^2 (14.7 lb in^2). On Venus, the same area has a pressure of 600 kg (1,323 lbs). This is the pressure a diver would experience at 80 m (264 ft) beneath the sea.

Back-to-front

Venus rotates east to west, in the opposite direction to all the other planets. This means that the Sun rises in the west and sets in the east.

Amazing But True

There is so little water in the Martian atmosphere that if all of it was collected together it would fit into the Serpentine Lake, London.

Mountain high

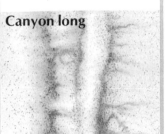

One of the highest mountains in the Solar System is found on Venus. It is called the Maxwell Montes and is more than 2 km (1.2 miles) higher than Mt. Everest.

Canyon long

Mars has the largest canyon in the Solar System, called the Mariner Valley. It is 13 times longer than the Grand Canyon in the USA and would stretch from one side of the USA to the other.

Midget moons

Mars has two tiny moons, called Phobos and Deimos. Deimos is so small and its gravity so weak that people could launch themselves into space by reaching a speed of 36 kph (22 mph).

Greenhouse effect

The atmosphere on Venus traps the heat rather like a greenhouse so that the temperature reaches about 500°C (932°F).

Jupiter and Saturn

Data	Jupiter	Saturn
Diameter at the equator	143,000 km	120,000 km
Mass	318 (Earth=1)	95
Orbital speed (round Sun)	13.1 km/sec	9.7 km/sec
Cloud top temperatures	–150°C	–180°C
Number of satellites	16	21

Sizing up Jupiter

Jupiter is much smaller than the Sun. If the Sun's diameter was equal to a giant tractor tyre 175 cm (69 in) in diameter, then Jupiter would be the size of a ball 18 cm (7 in) in diameter and the Earth would be the size of a small marble about 1 cm (0.4 in) in diameter.

Similar planets

Jupiter and Saturn are members of a group of four planets, known as the "gas giants", which are very different from the inner planets. They have small rocky centres, surrounded by liquid hydrogen and covered with thick, cloudy atmospheres.

The giant planet

Jupiter is the largest planet in our Solar System. Jupiter is more than 1,300 times bigger than Earth and bigger than all the other planets put together.

The Great Red Spot

The reddish patch on Jupiter is known as the Great Red Spot and was first recorded in the 17th century. It is the biggest hurricane in the Solar System with swirling clouds about 38,500 km (24,000 miles) long by 11,000 km (7,000 miles) wide. It is as big as three Earths.

Fat stomach

Jupiter spins round very quickly on its axis, taking less than 10 hours to make one turn. This forces the equator to bulge out so that the planet looks like a squashed ball.

Heart pressure

The core of Jupiter is about the size of Earth and has a temperature of about 30,000°C (54,000°F). The pressure at the core is more than 30 million times higher than the Earth's atmosphere. If anyone flew to Jupiter and then landed on the surface, they would be crushed by the pressure straight away.

Jupiter is so big that if a bicyclist set out to travel non-stop once round it at a speed of 9.6 kph (6 mph), the journey would take more than five years (1,935 days) to complete.

Inside-out moon

The most explosive object in the Solar System is one of Jupiter's moons, called Io. Geologists estimate that the volcanoes on its surface throw up enough material every 3,000 years to cover the entire surface with a thin layer about 1 cm (0.4 in) thick. So Io is continually turning itself inside out.

Speedy moon

The fastest-moving moon in the Solar System, known as J3, travels at a speed of about 113,600 km (70,400 miles) per hour. A person travelling at this speed could fly from Bombay in India to Port Said in Egypt in 2 minutes 11 seconds.

DID YOU KNOW?

Saturn is the second biggest planet in the Solar System and it is 95 times heavier than Earth. The volume of Saturn is 744 times that of Earth.

Hurricane winds

The winds that blow round Saturn's equator are ten-times stronger than the average hurricane on Earth, travelling at 1,770 kph (1,100 mph).

Record rings

Saturn is one of the most beautiful planets in the Solar System. It is surrounded by rings made up of millions of icy particles. The ice particles are like tiny mirrors and are very thin compared to their 275,000 km (171,000 miles) diameter. They are only about 100 m (300 ft) thick. On this scale, a gramaphone record 1.5 mm (0.06 in) thick would be 4 km (2.5 miles) across.

Lighter than water

Saturn is composed mostly of hydrogen and helium gas and liquid, like Jupiter. But it is smaller than Jupiter. It has the lowest density of all the planets in the Solar System. If it was the size of a tennis ball it would be able to float in a bucket of water.

Uranus, Neptune and Pluto

Data	Uranus	Neptune	Pluto
Diameter at the equator	52,000 km	49,000 km	Approx. 2,400 km
Mass	14.54 (Earth=1)	17.2	0.002?
Orbital speed round Sun	6.8 km/sec	5.4 km/sec	4.7 km/sec
Surface temperatures	–210°C	–220°C	–230°C
Satellites	15	2	1

Little and large

Uranus and Neptune are a second pair of "gas giants", though smaller than Jupiter and Saturn. Pluto is a small, solid planet, probably more like the rocky inner planets (Mercury, Venus, Earth and Mars). They are all far too cold for anything to live on their surfaces.

Green with methane

The atmospheres surrounding Uranus and Neptune contain hydrogen and helium, like those of Jupiter and Saturn. But their atmospheres also contain methane gas, which makes them look green from Earth.

Amazing But True

One of the strangest things about Uranus is that it rolls round the Sun on its side, while all the other planets spin round like tops. This means that either Uranus' northern or southern hemisphere

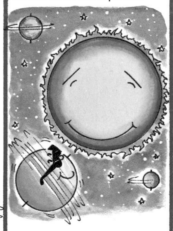

will face the Sun and will receive almost constant sunlight, while the other remains in darkness. This creates the Solar System's longest seasons, summers and winters about 21 years long.

New discovery

People used to think that the furthest planet in the Solar System was Saturn. But in 1781 an astronomer called Sir William Herschel discovered a faint planet which was later named Uranus. It was the first planet to be discovered since the Ancient Greeks.

Blacker than black

In 1977, astronomers discovered that Uranus has a set of narrow rings. There are now thought to be 10 of these. They are made of about the darkest material known in the Solar System.

Not quite a twin

Neptune was first seen in 1846. It is almost the twin of Uranus, but it is slightly smaller and it does not have Uranus' tilt. *

Uranus

Neptune

Old first birthday

A baby born on Pluto (if that was possible) would have to wait 147 Earth years before it reached its first birthday.

Long plane journey

The average distance of Neptune from the Sun is 4,500 million km (2,800 million miles). This is 30 times the distance between Earth and the Sun. If an aeroplane flew at 1,770 kph (1,100 mph), it would take 289 years to travel from Neptune to the Sun.

DID YOU KNOW?

A person on Neptune would never live for one Neptune year. The Neptune year is the time it takes Neptune to travel once round the Sun – 164.8 Earth years.

The smallest planet

Pluto was discovered in 1930. With a diameter of 2,400 km (1,500 miles) it is smaller than our Moon, making it the smallest and lightest planet in the Solar System.

Stretched orbit

Pluto has a very strange path round the Sun. While the routes of the other planets are almost circles, Pluto's is more elongated. Because of its strange orbit, Pluto is closer to the Sun between 1979 and 1999 than Neptune, making Neptune the furthest planet from Earth during those years.

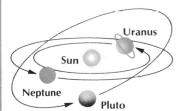

Uranus

Sun

Neptune

Pluto

Cosy companion

Pluto has a very close companion, a moon called Charon which was discovered in 1978 and which lies only 20,000 km (12,500 miles) from Pluto. Its diameter is about 800 km (500 miles), making it the largest moon compared to its planet in the Solar System.

Spaced out

For most of the time, Pluto is the furthest planet from Earth. An aeroplane travelling at a speed of 1,810 kph (1,125 mph) would take about 370 years to travel from Earth to Pluto.

*In 1989 the satellite Voyager 2 discovered rings around Neptune which are not visible from earth, even through a powerful telescope.

Asteroids, comets and meteors

Stone belt

Between the inner planets (Mercury, Venus, Earth and Mars) and the outer planets (Jupiter, Saturn, Uranus, Neptune and Pluto) lies a belt of about 40,000 much smaller irregular planets known as asteroids.

The main comets	
Name	Orbital period round Sun (years)
Schwassmann – Wachmann	16.1
Halley	76.03
D'Arrest	6.2
Encke	3.3
Pons – Winnecke	6.3
Finlay	6.9
Faye	7.4
Tuttle	13.61
Crommelin	27.9

Big lump

The largest asteroid is called Ceres. It measures about 1,000 km (620 miles) in diameter and if it arrived on Earth it could fit on to the surface of France.

Dirty snowballs

Comets are balls of icy particles and dust that come from the furthest parts of the Solar System and travel round the Sun. A comet glows slightly and reflects the light of the Sun. Scientists think that about 100,000 million comets may circle the Sun.

Roaring tail

When a comet approaches the Sun, a huge tail appears behind it. This is made up of gas and dust released from the comet by the heat of the Sun. The comet's tail points away from the Sun because the solar wind blows it away.

Wrapping up Earth

The Great Comet of 1843 had a tail about 330 million km (200 million miles) long. If this tail was wrapped round Earth it would circle the equator about 8,000 times.

Lighter than air

The density of a comet is far less than that of water or air. If all the comets were put together they would weigh no more than the Earth.

Life boat

According to astronomers Chandra Wickramasinghe and Sir Frederick Hoyle, life may have originated far out in space and been brought to Earth aboard a comet which crashed on to the surface.

Signs in the sky

The appearance of Halley's Comet in the sky through the centuries has been regarded as an important sign. It was seen in England in 1066 before the Battle of Hastings and William the Conqueror's battle cry was "A new star, a new king".

Streaking rocks

Meteors are small pieces of rock that enter the top of Earth's atmosphere. They do not manage to travel far down and reach the Earth's surface, but burn up about 80 km (50 miles) up in the sky, producing streaks of light known as "shooting stars".

Jumbo meteorite

Meteorites are large chunks of rock that reach the Earth's surface without burning up. Scientists think that they come from asteroids. The largest known meteorite in the world fell to Earth at Hoba West in Namibia, Africa. It measures 2.7x2.4 m (9x8 ft) and weighs about 60 tonnes, as much as 9 elephants.

Explosive impact

One of the most famous meteorite craters on Earth is the Arizona Crater in the USA. It was formed about 22,000 years ago and the force of the explosion when the meteorite hit Earth equalled 1,000 Hiroshima atomic bombs.

Iron from space

Eskimos in Greenland used iron tools for centuries, even though they could not smelt iron. They mined iron in almost pure form from three large meteorites that had fallen on Greenland hundreds of years ago.

DID YOU KNOW?

Meteors burn up in the atmosphere and filter down to Earth as dust. The total weight of the Earth increases in weight from this dust by about 25 tonnes each day, which adds up to 9,125 tonnes each year.

The life of stars

Millions of suns

The stars you can see in the night sky are really distant suns. Our Sun is only one very ordinary star among millions of others. The next nearest star to our Solar System is called Proxima Centauri and is 4.25 light years away.

A star is born

Stars are born from the huge clouds of gas and dust known as nebulae that float in the Universe. They begin to grow when part of a cloud forms into a small lump. This grows smaller and hotter until a nuclear reaction starts and the star is born.

DID YOU KNOW?

The longest name for any star is "Shurnarkabtishashutu", the Arabic for "under the southern horn of the bull".

Long journey

A car travelling from our Solar System at 88.5 kph (55 mph) would take 52 million years to drive to Proxima Centauri. This is equal to about 722,000 average lifetimes.

Hot heart

The heart of a star is extremely hot and reaches a temperature of about 16 million °C (29 million °F). A grain of sand that hot would kill a person up to 161 km (100 miles) away.

Long-distance call

One of the largest stars known is called Betelgeuse. It has a diameter of 1,000 million km (621 million miles), or about 730 times greater than the Sun. If you made a telephone call from one side to the other, your voice, travelling at the speed of light, would take 55 minutes to reach the other end of the line.

What is a star?

A star shines with its own light. It is made up mostly of hydrogen gas and held together by its own gravity. Reactions in the heart of stars, like those in nuclear bombs, generate heat and light.

Star death

When the hydrogen gas at the centre of a star is burned up, it begins to die. It then swells up to a red giant star. When our Sun begins to die it will swell up until it is beyond the Earth's orbit, destroying the entire planet and destroying Mercury and Venus as well.

Little heavyweight

A red giant star then collapses into a ball about the size of the Earth. This is known as a white dwarf star and its gravity is so strong that a large cupful of its material weighs about 500 tonnes, which is about the weight of two Boeing 747 jumbo jets put together.

Neutron stars

If a star is much bigger than the Sun, the collapse goes beyond the white dwarf stage and does not stop until the star is about 10 km (6.25 miles) across. This is called a neutron star and a pinhead of its material would weigh about 1 million tonnes. This is about the same weight as two of the world's largest supertankers put together.

Amazing But True

A 4 kg (9 lb) baby would weigh 40,000 million kg (90,000 million lb) on the surface of a neutron star because the gravity is so strong.

Pulsating stars

Some neutron stars spin round very fast, as much as 642 times a second, sending out a beam of radio waves. This type of neutron star is called a pulsar. The first pulsar was discovered in 1968 by a British astronomer called Antony Hewish. He thought it was a message coming from another planet, until more were discovered.

Shrinking to nothing

A dying star at least three times bigger than the Sun goes on shrinking beyond the neutron star stage. Its gravity is so strong that it drags everything back to the star. The star has become a black hole. Black holes are impossible to see because even light cannot escape from them.

Groups of stars

Star families

Some of the stars in our galaxy, like our Sun, are alone with no star companions. But because stars are normally born in groups which gradually drift apart, many are found in pairs or sometimes larger numbers.

Pairs of stars

Double, or binary, stars consist of two stars which circle round each other. Close pairs of stars may take only a day or even less to complete their circuits, but pairs that are far apart may take over a hundred years.

Star clusters

As well as binary stars and small groups, there are larger groups called star clusters. There are two types of cluster, known as open and globular. Open clusters are found in the spiral arms of our galaxy and usually contain several hundred young stars. Globular clusters are found near the centre of our galaxy and are much more compact groups containing up to a million older stars.

The Seven Sisters

About 1,000 open cluste are in our galaxy. The Pleiades is one such cluster, containing about 400 stars. It is also known as the Seven Sisters and can easily be found in the night sky without a telescope.

Amazing But True

There are about 120 globular clusters in our galaxy. Globular clusters are so tightly packed at their centres that if our Earth was placed in the middle of one the nearest stars would only be light days away, rather than light years. Our night sky would always be as bright as if there was a full moon shining.

The heaviest giants

Plaskett's star, lying about 2,700 light years away from us, is really made up of two giant stars that orbit each other every 14 days. Astronomers think that the largest of the two stars is so big that it is about 55 times heavier than the Sun. A star this weight would be the size of about 18 million Earths or 1,460 million Moons.

A gang of stars

As well as double stars, there are star systems with three or even more members, though not many of these are known. A well-known example, called Castor, contains six stars. Only three stars can be seen with a telescope, two bright and one dim, but each is really a close double star.

DID YOU KNOW?

A nova (meaning "new star") is a star that suddenly flares up to be many times brighter than it was. A really brilliant nova may have been a star which could hardly be seen even with a large telescope. It then suddenly becomes visible to the naked eye but gradually fades again.

Eclipsing stars

Some pairs of stars move round each other so that, seen from Earth, they block out each other's light. These are known as eclipsing binaries and the amount of light we can see goes down during each eclipse.

Mystery giant

One of the most mysterious eclipsing binary stars is called Epsilon Aurigae. The two stars revolve round each other every 27 years. One of the stars has never been directly seen but some astronomers believe it may be the largest star known, with a diameter 2,800 times that of the Sun. If it was placed in the middle of our Solar System, the edge of this star would reach as far as Uranus.

Throbbing stars

Eclipsing stars are not the only ones whose brightness goes up and down. There are some stars called the Cepheid variables that actually swell and shrink regularly. As they throb in and out their brightness also rises and falls.

The brightest star

Eta Carinae is an unusual variable star. Astronomers think that it may be a slow nova star. In 1843 it flashed its record brilliance which has been estimated to have been up to six million times brighter than the Sun, making Eta Carinae the most brilliant star ever recorded.

Nebulae

Dusty space

Although the stars in the night sky look close together, they are really separated by huge stretches of space. This space contains very small gas and dust particles known as interstellar matter.

Interstellar matter is much thinner than the air we breathe on Earth. A cup of air contains about 1,000 million, million, million atoms, but a cupful of space gas is so thin that it would contain only about 300 atoms.

Gas and dust clouds

Some of the interstellar matter in space has collected together to form clouds called nebulae (from the Latin for clouds). There are three types of nebula.

Dark nebulae do not shine but, by blocking out the light from the stars behind, they appear as darker patches in the sky.

Reflection nebulae also do not shine but reflect the light from nearby stars.

Many glowing nebulae contain young, hot stars which make the gases glow.

Star nurseries

The oldest stars in our galaxy are concentrated in the central bulge. The younger stars, like our Sun, lie further from the centre in the spiral arms. This is the area where stars are born and objects like the Orion, Lagoon and Trifid nebulae are star birthplaces. The dark spots inside may be baby stars.

Galactic babies

Every 18 days, about 20 times a year, our galaxy gives birth to a new star. Every half second a human birth occurs on Earth.

Giant explosions

Some nebulae are formed from the remains of giant star explosions called supernovae. The outer layers of the star are thrown off as clouds of gas which glow. The Crab Nebula is the most famous example of this type and is believed to have been formed in 1054, when Edward the Confessor was King of England.

Super-cloud

The Orion Nebula is so huge that if the distance between the Earth and the Sun was represented by 2.5 cm (1 in), the Orion Nebula would be 20.3 km (12.6 miles) in diameter.

Blowing bubbles

A huge cloud of gas called the Cygnus Superbubble lies about 6,500 light years away from our Solar System. Astronomers believe that this superbubble was formed from a number of supernovae explosions over the last three or four million years.

Death and life

Supernovae explosions are so powerful that they are brighter than 1,000 million Suns. This type of nebula represents the end of a star's life and new stars will be born from the clouds of gas to continue the cycle of life and death.

A veil of gas

The Veil Nebula lies about 2,500 light years away from us and is probably formed from the remains of a supernova explosion. Astronomers have worked out that the explosion took place about 50,000 years ago, when primitive humans lived on Earth.

Amazing But True

The Orion Nebula in our galaxy is a glowing nebula. It lies about 1,600 light years away from us but it is so bright that it can be seen with the naked eye. It is many times thinner than the air we breathe. If a sample 2.5 cm (1 in) in diameter could be taken all the way through the nebula, the material collected would weigh less than a small coin.

Smoke signals

Ring nebulae are formed from the puffs of gases given off by dying stars when they reach the red giant stage near the end of their lifetimes. The expanding, glowing gases form rings round the stars.

The Milky Way

Our galaxy

Stars are not scattered randomly throughout the Universe, but are grouped together in giant clouds known as galaxies. The Milky Way is the name of the galaxy our Solar System lies in, in one of the spiral arms.

Star town

The Milky Way contains at least 100,000 million stars. Huge distances lie between each one. If each star was the size of the full-stop at the end of this sentence, there would be one star every 21 cm^2 (3.26 in^2), covering an area of about 40 km (15.5 square miles). This is the size of a small town.

Giant catherine wheel

Because we live inside the Milky Way, it is difficult to see its shape. Astronomers have worked out that the Milky Way is in the shape of a giant spiral measuring about 100,000 light years in diameter. Two starry arms wind round the centre several times like a catherine wheel.

DID YOU KNOW?

The word galaxy comes from the Greek word for milk, "gala". The Ancient Greeks thought the Milky Way was formed from spilt milk from the breast of the goddess Hera when she suckled the baby Herakles (Hercules).

Pot belly

The centre of the Milky Way measures about 20,000 light years from one side to the other and bulges up and down. About 40,000 million of the galaxy's stars are concentrated in the centre.

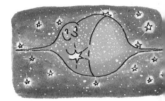

Star crashes

Stars at the centre of the Milky Way probably collide once every 1,000 years. If the car collision rate on Earth was the same we would have to wait two million years before the first crash, and there would not have been a single one so far in car history.

Cutting it down to size

If our Solar System could fit into a tea cup, the Milky Way would be the size of North America.

Galactic fog

We cannot see deep into the heart of the Milky Way because of huge clouds of gas and dust that block the view. To see the centre from Earth would be like trying to see the Moon through a thick cloud of smoke.

Greedy guts

Some astronomers think that a very powerful black hole lies at the centre of the Milky Way, equal in weight to four million Suns. Such a black hole would be so powerful that it would capture and destroy the equivalent of 3.3 Earths every year.

Galaxy drive

Our Solar System lies in one of the arms of the Milky Way, about 33,000 light years from the centre of the galaxy. If you drove a car from Earth at 161 km (100 miles) per hour it would take a total of about 221,000 million years to reach the centre of the Milky Way.

Amazing But True

Our galaxy is so huge that a flash of light travelling at its natural speed of 1,100 million km (670 million miles) per hour would take 100,000 years to go from one side of the galaxy to the other.

Changing shape

The stars of the Milky Way move continuously round the centre, but they do not turn like a solid wheel. Stars near the centre travel one circuit in only 10 million years, yet out near our Solar System a single

circuit takes about 225 million years. Every time our Solar System moves once round the galaxy, the central stars turn 100 times. This means that the shape of the Milky Way is changing slowly the whole time.

Happy cosmic birthday

A cosmic year is the time it takes our galaxy to cover one complete circuit, about 225 million years. One cosmic year ago, the Earth was at the beginning of the Triassic period, when giant reptiles were replacing sea creatures as the main form of life.

Galaxies

A drop in the ocean of space

Most astronomers believe that galaxies were formed about 14,000 million years ago, about 1,000 million years after the Big Bang (the explosion that formed the Universe). The galaxy we live in is called the Milky Way. There are probably thousands of millions of other galaxies.

The Earth is the third closest planet to the Sun and one of the smaller planets of the Solar System.

The Solar System is tiny when seen in its galaxy, the Milky Way.

The Milky Way itself is insignificant when pictured with the other galaxies.

Types of galaxies

Galaxies come in various shapes. Four main types have been named according to their shapes: spirals, ellipticals, barred spirals and irregular galaxies.

The largest galaxies have diameters of about 500,000 light years but the smallest have diameters of a few thousand light years.

Spiral

Elliptical

Barred spiral

Irregular

DID YOU KNOW?

Galaxies are found in groups or clusters. Many clusters of galaxies are known, some of which contain hundreds of members loosely held together by the force of gravity. The Virgo cluster of galaxies, more than 60 million light years away from us, contains at least 1,000 galaxies. Our cluster consists of only about 20 galaxies.

Carry on counting

An average galaxy contains about 100,000 million stars. To count all the stars would take a thousand years at the rate of three a second.

Outshining the Sun

The galaxy known as M87 is the brightest in the Virgo cluster. A mysterious jet of gases streams out of its centre about 5,000 light years into space. The brightest point in this jet shines with the strength of 40 million Suns.

Second-rate galaxy

Our galaxy, the Milky Way, is a member of a cluster known as the local group which contains about 20 other galaxies. A galaxy called the Andromeda Spiral is the largest member of the group, with the Milky Way coming a poor second.

Older than humans

The Andromeda Spiral is estimated to be 2.2 million light years from the Milky Way. It is the most distant object visible to the naked eye, yet it is still one of the nearest galaxies to us. When you look at Andromeda you are seeing light that started its journey towards you when mammoths first lived on the Earth's surface.

Amazing But True

Some galaxies are powerful sources of radio waves as well as light. These are known as radio galaxies. Astronomers now think that the radio waves could be caused by huge explosions inside the galaxies.

Calling all quasars

In 1963 radio waves were discovered to be coming from objects that looked like faint stars. These are now called quasars and about 1,300 have so far been discovered. They seem to be small compared to galaxies but up to a thousand times brighter than normal galaxies.

To the edge of time

The most distant object ever seen in the Universe through a telescope is a quasar known as PKS2000-330 and it is thought to be 13,000 million light years away from us. It is racing

away from our galaxy at a speed of about 273,000 km/sec (170,000 miles/sec), about two-thirds the distance from the Earth to the Moon each second.

Origins of the Universe

The Big Bang theory

Most astronomers now believe that the Universe began with a huge explosion, often referred to as the "Big Bang". A tiny point of incredible energy blew apart, scattering hot gases in every direction. Out of this material the galaxies, stars and planets were formed.

Disappearing stars

When their light is examined with special equipment, most stars show something known as red shift. This indicates that the stars are moving away from us and shows that the Universe is still expanding with the force of the Big Bang. When the Universe was 9.5 million years old, it was expanding at nearly the speed of light – 300,000 km (186,000 miles) per second.

The age of the Universe

Once astronomers had measured the speed at which the galaxies are moving outwards, they could work backwards to decide how long ago the Universe began. They now generally agree that it started about 15,000 million years ago. If each year was equal to one second the seconds would add up to almost 475 years.

Time chart

Millions of years		Event
0		Big Bang
1,000		Galaxies begin to form.
4,000		Stars develop within galaxies.
10,000		Our Solar System forms.
11,000		Life begins to form on Earth.
14,650		Human beings (Homo sapiens) first appear on Earth.
15,000		Today

A hot pinhead

Astronomers think that the temperature one second after the Big Bang was so hot that it measured about 10,000 million °C. Just a pinhead amount of this very high temperature, with a radius of 1 mm (0.03937 in), would equal over 18 times the entire energy output of the Sun since it was born about 5,000 million years ago.

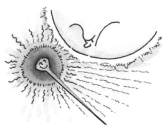

Radio astronomers used to think that the crackling noises picked up on their equipment were caused by pigeon droppings on their radio antennae. But they have now found that space is filled with faint radio waves. These are the dying radio echoes of the Big Bang.

Starting all over again

Some astronomers believe that the outward-speeding galaxies could slow down and then fall back towards the centre. Finally they would collide and create a new explosion. The cycle would be repeated about every 80,000 million years, which means that the next Big Bang could take place in about 65,000 million years' time. This is known as the Oscillating Universe theory.

Staying the same

Some astronomers believe that although the Universe is expanding it always looks the same. This is because new galaxies are formed at the centre to replace those that are moving outwards. This is known as the Steady State theory.

Some of the particles that make up living things have been found in outer space. One of them is alcohol. Astronomers estimate that a huge cloud in the constellation of Sagittarius contains enough ethyl alcohol to make 10,000 million, million, million, million bottles of whisky.

The mysterious neutrino

Among the most mysterious ingredients of the Universe are neutrinos. They are unimaginably tiny particles, freed one second after the Big Bang. These particles travel at the speed of light and can pass right through Earth without even slowing down. Millions will pass through this page, and through you, in the time it takes you to read it.

Early astronomy

Farming astronomers

People in ancient times used the position of the Sun and the Moon in the skies to tell them the season of the year, so that they could plan the planting and harvesting of their crops. They built stone monuments thousands of years ago that served as giant calendars, some of which can still be seen in parts of the world today.

Stone calendar

Stonehenge in England was started nearly 4,000 years ago and has different pairs of stones which can be lined up with sunrise and moonrise on different days throughout the year. This monument may have been used to find midsummer and midwinter before the invention of the calendar.

A giant clock

The Great Pyramid of Cheops was built by the Ancient Egyptians in about 2,550BC. It is probably the world's oldest astronomical observatory and as well as being a tomb it was designed to tell the time in hours, days, seasons and even centuries.

Nearly right

The distance around the Earth was first accurately measured by a Greek astronomer called Eratosthenes, who lived from about 276 to 194BC. His figure of about 40,000 km (24,856 miles) almost matched the modern measurement of 40,007 km (24,860 miles).

Using a telescope

In the early 17th century, the Italian scientist Galileo Galilei was the first person to use a telescope in astronomy. Among his discoveries, he first saw four of Jupiter's moons and argued that the planets circled the Sun in the same way as these moons circled Jupiter.

DID YOU KNOW?

The first person to claim that the Earth revolves round the Sun was a Greek astronomer called Aristarchos of Samos, who lived from about 310 to 250BC. But as everyone believed the Sun moved round the Earth, this idea was not accepted.

The Ptolemaic theory

In about AD150, a Greek astronomer known as Ptolemy stated that the Earth lay stationary at the centre of the Universe and the Sun, the Moon and the five known planets (Mercury, Venus, Mars, Jupiter and Saturn) all moved round it. Most people believed this for the next 1,400 years.

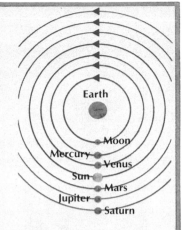

The Copernican theory

In 1543, a Polish clergyman called Nicolas Copernicus stated that the Sun was at the centre of the Universe and not the Earth. The Earth turned on its axis once a day and travelled round the Sun once a year. But Copernicus still believed that the planets moved round in circles, which is wrong.

Going round in ellipses

Finally, in 1609, Johannes Kepler of Germany worked out the correct movement of the planets. He calculated that the planets moved round the Sun in ellipses (flattened circles) not circles.

The world is round

In the 6th century BC, the Greek mathematician Pythagoras claimed that the Earth was a sphere rotating on its axis. But most people thought that the Earth was flat and so few agreed with him.

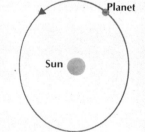

The pull of gravity

The story that the English astronomer Sir Isaac Newton worked out his Law of Universal Gravity in 1687 after watching an apple fall to the ground is probably true. He realized that the force which pulled down the apple was the same as the force which keeps the Moon in its path round the Earth and all the planets in their paths round the Sun.

Amazing But True

In the 6th century BC a Greek philosopher called Heraclitus estimated that the Sun measured only about one-third of a metre (1 ft) across. In fact, it is nearly 1.4 million km (870,000 miles) across.

Modern astronomy

Above the clouds

Many astronomers today work in large observatories built high in mountain ranges. Here they are above most of the clouds and away from the dazzle of street lights so that they can see the night sky more clearly.

Amazing But True

A telescope in the Lick Observatory, USA also serves as a tomb. The refracting telescope is mounted on a pillar that contains the remains of James Lick, who paid for the observatory and who died in 1876.

Increasing the light

Astronomers can see many thousands of stars that are invisible to the naked eye by using telescopes. These are used to magnify distant objects, such as nebulae, and also to collect more light coming from them and reaching the eye.

Lenses and mirrors

Telescopes collect light from stars using either a lens (a refracting telescope) or a mirror (a reflecting telescope). The larger the lens or mirror in a telescope, the more light it can collect and so the more powerful it is. The largest modern telescopes are usually reflectors.

The big one

The world's largest reflecting telescope was built in the 1970s near Zelenchukskaya in the Caucasus Mountains, USSR. Its largest mirror weighs 70 tonnes and measures 6 m (236 in) across. It is powerful enough to spot the light from a single candle 24,000 km (15,000 miles) away.

Odd one out

One of the strangest telescopes is buried 1,500 m (1 mile) down a mine in South Dakota, USA. At the bottom is a tank containing 400,000 litres (88,000 gallons) of tetrachloroethylene (cleaning fluid). This is used to stop neutrinos, tiny particles given off by the Sun, so that they can be counted by astronomers.

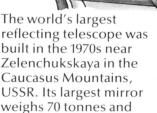

Giant cameras

Photographs of stars and planets were first taken through a telescope in 1840. Photography is now so important in astronomy that many observatories have telescopes which have been designed not to be looked through and can only take photographs.

Colour information

In the 19th century, astronomers first began to study the light from the Sun and stars by splitting it up into its different colours. This is known as spectroscopy. From the colours astronomers can tell the temperature and types of gases in the stars and so what the stars are made of.

Radio telescopes

Radio telescopes are designed to pick up radio waves coming from distant radio sources. The first true radio telescope was built in 1937. The main type of radio telescope today looks like a giant dish. The radio waves are focused on to the telescope's receiver, above or below the dish.

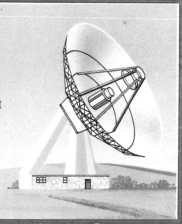

Some radio telescopes, known as interferometers, consist of two or more medium-sized radio telescopes. This is like using a single radio dish several kilometres wide and so gives a much clearer picture of the skies.

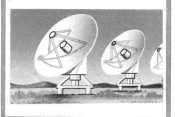

A faint glimmer

Radio waves from space are very weak. It has been calculated that if the energy reaching us from a quasar – a mysterious type of galaxy that sends out radio waves – were collected by a radio telescope for 10,000 years, there would only be enough to light a small bulb for a fraction of a second.

The sensitive giant

The world's largest radio telescope is at Arecibo in Puerto Rico. Its dish measures 305 m (1,000 ft) across, wider than three football fields. It can pick up signals as weak as one-hundredth of a millionth of a millionth of a watt. (An ordinary light bulb is 100 watts.)

Astronomy in orbit

Blanket atmosphere

A lot of information from stars never reaches astronomers on the ground because of the blanket of atmosphere that surrounds the Earth. Now that telescopes can be placed above the atmosphere, astronomers can detect invisible waves of energy from stars known as ultra-violet and X-rays which never reach the Earth's surface.

Light bulb power

Most satellites are powered by solar cells, which convert sunlight into electricity. On average, a scientific satellite needs only about 250 watts of power. This is about the amount of power used in two ordinary house light bulbs.

Eyes in the sky

Before satellites carrying telescopes were launched into space, there were three ways of looking at the stars from above the Earth's surface – from aeroplanes, balloons and rockets. These are all still used, as well as satellites.

Homes in the sky

A space station is a kind of giant satellite where people can live for many days on end without returning to Earth. The Russian Salyut and the latest Mir series and the American Skylab were launched to carry out scientific experiments and to discover the effect on people of long periods in space.

What they can see

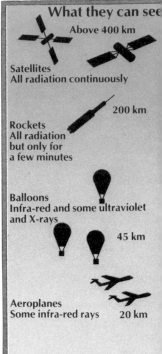

Above 400 km

Satellites
All radiation continuously

200 km

Rockets
All radiation but only for a few minutes

Balloons
Infra-red and some ultraviolet and X-rays

45 km

Aeroplanes
Some infra-red rays   20 km

Observatories
Visible light and radio waves

4.5 km

A long time in space

The longest time anyone has spent non-stop in space is nearly 237 days. This was achieved in 1984 by three Russian cosmonauts called Kizim, Solovyov and Atkov in Salyut 7.

The first space station

The first space station, called Salyut 1, was launched by Russia in 1971. Salyut 6 spent five years in space, the longest time a space station has spent in orbit. It re-entered the Earth's atmosphere and broke up in 1982.

DID YOU KNOW?

In space, far from the pull of gravity of planets, objects have no weight. This is known as weightlessness. People get a little taller in space because the discs in their backbones are no longer squashed down by the pressure of gravity and their backs stretch a little.

As big as a house

The total size of Skylab, with the Apollo Command and Service modules attached, was about 331.5 cu m (11,700 cu ft), about the same as a small, two-bedroom house.

Spinning and swimming

Small animals were also kept on board Skylab. Two spiders adapted to weightlessness and spun normal webs. Minnows born on Earth swam in a tank in small circles, but those born in space swam normally.

The space ferry

The Space Shuttle is designed mainly as a ferry to carry people and equipment such as satellites into space. The cost of the entire shuttle programme so far, $9,900 million, amounts to about $2 for every human being in the world.

Amazing But True

The space telescope is so accurate that if it was placed on Earth it could see a small coin 700 km (435 miles) away. This is about the distance between London, England and Basle, Switzerland. The space telescope should also be able to see if there are any planets circling nearby stars in our galaxy.

The space telescope

The USA is planning to launch a telescope into space using the Space Shuttle. The space telescope will orbit about 600 km (373 miles)

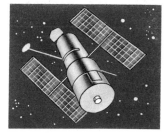

above the Earth and is designed to detect objects 50 times fainter or seven times further away than anything which can be seen from Earth.

Missions to the Moon

Orbiting football

Sputnik 1 was launched by the Russians in October 1957 and was the first spacecraft to go into orbit round the Earth. This marks the real beginning of the Space Age and the race to reach the Moon. Sputnik 1 weighed only 84 kg (185 lb), about the weight of an adult, and was the size of a large ball.

Unmanned probes

Spacecraft	Date	Results
Luna 2 (USSR)	12 Sep 59	First man-made object to hit the Moon.
Luna 3 (USSR)	4 Oct 59	Flew behind the Moon and took the first photographs of the far side.
Rangers (USA)	1964-65	Photographed the Moon before crashing into the surface.
Luna 9 (USSR)	31 Jan 66	Made the first soft-landing on the Moon and sent back photographs.
Surveyors (USA)	1966-68	Collected information about the surface of the Moon in preparation for manned landings.
Orbiters (USA)	1966-67	Photographed the Moon's surface for possible landing sites.
Luna 16 (USSR)	12 Sep 70	Made soft-landing, collected soil and returned it to USSR.
Luna 17 (USSR)	10 Nov 70	Landed Lunokhod 1, a roving vehicle for experiments controlled from Earth. It travelled for nearly a year.

Flying high

On April 12th 1961, the Russian astronaut Yuri Gagarin became the first person to travel in space. His spacecraft, called Vostok, circled Earth once, reaching a height of 327 km (203 miles), and then landed on Earth again. The flight lasted about 89 minutes and proved that people could travel in space.

Off target

A mistake of only 1.6 kph (1 mph) in the Apollo's top speed would have led to it missing the Moon by about 1,600 km (1,000 miles). This is about the distance between Moscow and Berlin.

DID YOU KNOW?

The first living creature in space was a dog called Laika, launched in a spacecraft by the USSR in 1957. It died when its oxygen ran out.

A year in space

The world's most travelled person is the Russian astronaut Valery Ryumin. His total time in space is 362 days, nearly a year. During his space trips he went round the world 5,750 times, covering 241 million km (150 million miles), more than the distance from Earth to Mars and back again.

Man on the Moon		
Spacecraft	**Date**	**Results**
Apollo 11 (USA)	16-24 July 69	Landed the first man on the Moon.
Apollo 12 (USA)	12-24 Nov 69	32 hour stay on the Moon.
Apollo 13 (USA)	11-17 Apr 70	Explosion in the spacecraft. Astronauts returned to Earth before landing.
Apollo 14 (USA)	31 Jan-9 Feb 71	Highland area of the Moon explored.
Apollo 15 (USA)	26 July-7 Aug 71	A car called a Lunar Rover taken to the Moon. Astronauts travelled 28 km (17.4 miles).
Apollo 16 (USA)	16-27 Apr 72	Another Lunar Rover taken on mission.
Apollo 17 (USA)	7-19 Dec 72	The last and longest stay on the Moon.

Amazing But True

On Earth, an astronaut in his spacesuit weighs about 135 kg (300 lb). But on the Moon he is six times lighter at only 23 kg (50 lb) because the Moon has much less gravity than the Earth.

Big booster

The total power developed by the USA Saturn V booster rocket, used for all the Apollo missions to the Moon, was almost 4,082,000 kg (9,000,000 lb) of thrust. This is equal to the power of 50 Boeing 747 jumbo jets.

Lunar rubbish

The Apollo astronauts left the remains of six lunar landers, three lunar rover vehicles and more than 50 tonnes of litter on the Moon. The total cost of the Apollo missions to the Moon is estimated at $25,000 million, making this some of the most expensive rubbish in history.

Visiting the planets

Automatic equipment

Since 1962, America and Russia have been launching unmanned spacecaft to investigate the other planets in our Solar System. They carry cameras to take pictures and equipment to measure the magnetic fields and radiation of the planets. They also measure the temperature of the planets.

Probes to the planets

Spacecraft	Launch date	Mission
Mariner 2 (USA)	27 Aug 62	First successful fly-by of Venus.
Mariner 4 (USA)	28 Nov 64	First successful fly-by of Mars.
Venera 4 (USSR)	12 Jun 67	First entry into Venus atmosphere.
Mariner 9 (USA)	30 May 71	First successful Mars orbiter.
Pioneer 10 (USA)	3 Mar 72	First successful fly-by of Jupiter.
Venera 8 (USSR)	27 Mar 72	Returned first data from Venus surface.
Pioneer 11 (USA)	6 Apr 73	Jupiter probe. First fly-by of Saturn.
Mariner 10 (USA)	3 Nov 73	First TV pictures of Venus and Mercury.
Venera 9 (USSR)	8 Jun 75	First pictures from surface of Venus.
Viking 1 (USA)	20 Aug 75	First successful Mars landing.
Viking 2 (USA)	9 Sep 75	Returned data from Mars surface.
Voyager 2 (USA)	20 Aug 77	Fly-by of Jupiter, Saturn, Uranus, Neptune.
Voyager 1 (USA)	5 Sep 77	Fly-by probe of Jupiter and Saturn.
Pioneer-Venus 1 (USA)	20 May 78	Orbited Venus.
Pioneer-Venus 2 (USA)	8 Aug 78	Analysed atmosphere and clouds of Venus.
Venera 13 (USSR)	30 Oct 81	First colour pictures of Venus surface. First soil analysis.
Venera 14 (USSR)	4 Nov 81	Repeated Venus soil analysis.
Venera 15 (USSR)	June 1983	Orbited and mapped Venus surface.
Venera 16 (USSR)	June 1983	Orbited and mapped Venus surface.

A clearer picture

Mariner 10 took about 4,300 close-up photographs of Mercury during its three visits from 1974. Before this, telescopes on Earth could hardly see the surface of Mercury.

Amazing But True

Voyager 1 passed Saturn's moon Titan at a distance of only 4,000 km (2,500 miles) from the surface. It was more than 1,524 million km (946 million miles) from Earth. Such accuracy is like shooting an arrow at an apple 9.6 km (6 miles) away and the arrow passing within 2.54 cm (1 in) of the apple.

Goodbye

Pioneer 10 is expected to become the first man-made object to leave our Solar System. It crossed Neptune's path in 1983 and it will eventually disappear into the depths of space.

Metal message

Pioneer 10 and 11 carry metal plaques with messages for any aliens that might intercept the probes. Each plaque shows a map of the Solar System, the location of our Sun and sketches of human beings.

Look out

In 1968 a piece of Russian rocket broke a house window in Southend-on-Sea, Essex, England. In 1978 two French farmers were nearly hit by a 20 kg (44 lb) piece of a Russian rocket which landed in a field.

Six hour fly-by

The Voyager spacecraft travelled under Saturn's ring system at almost 69,000 kph (43,000 mph). At this speed, a rocket would take just six hours to travel from the Earth to the Moon. This is about the time it takes to travel from London to Bahrain by jet aeroplane today.

DID YOU KNOW?

By 1990 there will be about 7,000 pieces of space debris orbiting the Earth, consisting of discarded rocket stages and fragments of rockets and satellites that have broken up.

Mapping it out

In less than two years from 1978, the Pioneer-Venus spacecraft mapped 93 per cent of Venus' surface. More was mapped of Venus in that time than had been mapped of Earth up to the year 1800.

Making music

Voyager 1 and 2 carry long-playing records containing electronically coded pictures of the Earth, spoken greetings, sound effects and a selection of music from around the world.

183

The future in space

A new space age

The human race is about to enter a new age of travelling and living in space. Shuttles will one day make journeys into space as common as ordinary aeroplane flights today. Space cities holding thousands of people will circle the Earth, metals will be mined and future wars may be fought in space.

Living on the Moon

By the beginning of the next century, the first bases on the Moon with people living in them should have been started. Because of the expense of transporting goods to the Moon, edible plants will have to be grown on it and as many things as possible, such as water, oxygen and rubbish, will have to be recycled.

Space cities

Plans have been suggested for building giant colonies in space, housing thousands of people. The land areas would be on the inside surfaces of giant cylinders or wheels which would spin round to provide gravity similar to the Earth's. Inside, people could walk around as freely as on Earth and grow their own food.

Terraforming Mars

Some scientists believe that the atmosphere of Mars could be warmed up so that people could live and work there. In a process called terraforming, plants would be grown round the ice caps to absorb sunlight, warm the surface and melt the ice.

Greening the galaxy

One day special trees might be developed so that they can grow on comets. Seeds from the trees could drift across space to take root on other comets, starting a wave of "greening" throughout the galaxy so that human beings could live on distant planets.

Amazing But True

In order to supply Venus with water, some scientists believe that icy comets could be diverted into the carbon dioxide clouds that surround the planet. There they would be melted to make rivers and lakes.

Space factories

Materials such as special metals and glass and also some medicines that are impossible to make on Earth can be made in space because of the lack of gravity. Eventually whole industries may be moved from Earth and housed in the space cities.

First space product

The first product ever to be made in space and sold on Earth were tiny balls made of a type of rubber called latex and used to measure microscopic objects. They were all exactly the same size, but latex balls made on Earth can vary in size.

Energy from space

Some scientists believe that the Earth's electricity in the future could come from space. Giant groups of solar cells, which convert sunlight into electricity, would be placed about 35,880 km (22,300 miles) above the equator. The electricity generated by the solar cells would then be beamed down to Earth.

Mining in space

The world is beginning to run short of some essential metals and minerals such as iron and aluminium, but there are plentiful supplies of them elsewhere in the Solar System. One day our Moon and planets such as Mars and the asteroids will be mined for metals.

DID YOU KNOW?

Solar power stations would weigh at least 50,000 tonnes each, more than 600 times the weight of Skylab, the heaviest object ever launched into space. To build a power station in orbit round Earth would need about 5,000 flights of the Space Shuttle to carry the building materials.

Starships

The closest star to our Solar System is over four light years away. The journey in a rocket today would take nearly 200,000 years. Future rocket engines have been suggested that would use beams of light for power. These rockets could nearly reach the speed of light, so the same journey would take just over four years.

Is there life out there?

We are not alone

Some scientists believe that there are other civilizations in the Milky Way as well as ours. With about 100,000 million stars in our galaxy, it has been estimated that there may be up to one million planets on which there is life of some kind, such as animals or plants.

Am I receiving you?

In 1960, an American astronomer called Frank Drake made the first attempt to pick up possible messages from other stars. He turned a radio telescope towards two stars, called Tau Ceti and Epsilon Eridani. Although he listened for two months, Drake received no messages from the stars.

Strange sights

For centuries there have been reports of strange lights in the sky, craft landing on Earth and creatures emerging from them. Recently, sightings of UFOs (unidentified flying objects) have increased. Most are easily explained, but some remain mysteries.

Some famous UFOs

1254. A mysterious coloured ship is supposed to have appeared over St.Albans, England.

1741. Lord Beauchamp saw a small oval ball of fire descending from the sky in England. It then vanished.

1762. A thin UFO surrounded by a glowing ring was spotted by two astronomers near Basle, Switzerland.

1820. A stream of saucer-shaped objects crossed the town of Embrun, France.

1947. A pilot reported seeing gleaming discs flying over the Rocky Mountains, USA. He described them as "skipping like saucers across water" and the name "flying saucer" caught on.

1971. Two men in the USA claimed to have been captured and taken on board a flying saucer where they were examined by tall creatures.

Are you receiving me?

Since 1974, a radio message beamed from the Arecibo radio telescope in Puerto Rico has been racing towards a cluster of 300,000 stars known as M13. The stars are so far away that even if there are any creatures living in M13, their answer will not reach Earth until about the year 50,000.

The pattern of the Arecibo message

Amazing But True

Over the last 30 years over 100,000 people have reported UFO experiences. A public opinion poll carried out in the USA in 1974 showed that more than one in ten people questioned claimed to have seen a UFO.

A vintage year

1952 was a very good year for UFO sightings. There were about 1,500 reports of UFOs from different parts of the world. Most of these sightings have simple explanations, such as aeroplanes, clouds or bright stars, but many remain unexplained.

Swedish sightings

In 1946 in Sweden alone there were about 1,000 reports of UFOs. Most of the reports were of rocket-shaped objects, which have never been identified.

Lines in the sand

At Nazca in Peru there is a plain covered by very straight and wide tracks in the rocky surface up to 8 km (5 miles) long. Seen from above, they look like an airfield. They may be connected with early astronomy, but it is unlikely that they were used as runways by UFOs, as some people claim.

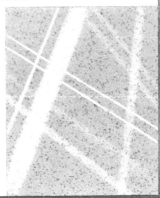

Putting up statues

Some people believe that the giant statues on Easter Island in the Pacific Ocean were put up with the help of visitors from space. But scientists believe that it would have been possible for the islanders to have erected them without any outside help.

DID YOU KNOW?

UFOs are usually seen between 9 pm and 10.30 pm. They have been reported from every country in the world. News of them flows in at an average of 40 sightings every day.

UFO spotting in space

The first UFO seen in space was spotted by the astronaut James McDivitt through the window of the Gemini 4 spacecraft in 1965. He saw an object with arms sticking out of it about 15 km (9.5 miles) from the capsule.

Astronomy lists

Famous observatories

Name	Country	Type
Arecibo	Puerto Rico	Radio
Byurakan	USSR	Optical
Cambridge	England	Radio
Cerro Tololo	Chile	Optical
Flagstaff	USA	Optical
Green Bank	USA	Radio
La Palma	Canary Islands	Optical
Jodrell Bank	England	Radio
Kitt Peak	USA	Optical
Mauna Kea	Hawaii	Optical
Mt Palomar	USA	Optical
Parkes	Australia	Radio
Pulkovo	USSR	Optical
Siding Spring	Australia	Optical
Zelenchukskaya	USSR	Optical

Meteor showers

Name	Date
Quadrantids	Jan 1-5
April Lyrids	Apr 19-24
Aquarids	May 1-8
June Lyrids	June 10-21
Perseids	July 25- Aug 18
Cygnids	Aug 18-22
Orionids	Oct 16-27
Taurids	Oct 10- Dec 5
Leonids	Nov 14-20
Geminids	Dec 7-15

The largest asteroids

Name	Diameter (km)
Ceres	1,000
Pallas	610
Vesta	540
Hygeia	450
Euphrosyne	370
Interamnia	350
Davida	330
Cybele	310
Europa	290
Patientia	280
Eunomia	270
Psyche	250

Future solar total eclipses

Date	Approximate location	Approximate duration
18 March 1988	Indian Ocean, North Pacific	4 minutes
22 July 1990	North Siberia	2 minutes
11 July 1991	Mexico, northern South America	7 minutes
30 June 1992	Uruguay, South Atlantic	5 minutes
3 Nov 1994	Central South America, South Atlantic	4 minutes
24 Oct 1995	South Asia, Central Pacific	2 minutes
9 March 1997	Central Asia	3 minutes
26 Feb 1998	Central Pacific, northern South America	4 minutes
11 Aug 1999	North Atlantic, Central Europe, South Asia	2 minutes

Our local group of galaxies

Leo I	NGC6822
Leo II	NGC185
Large Magellanic Cloud	IC1613
	Wolf-Lundmark
Sculptor	Triangulum
Fornax	NGC147
Milky Way	M32
Small Magellanic Cloud	Andromeda NGC205

Major astronomical satellites

OSO 1
7 March, 1962
Orbiting Solar
Observatory

OSO 2
3 Feb, 1965
Orbiting Solar
Observatory

OSO 3
8 March, 1967
Orbiting Solar
Observatory

OSO 4
18 Oct, 1967
Orbiting Solar
Observatory

OAO 2
7 Dec, 1968
Orbiting
Astronomical
Observatory, for
ultraviolet
observations

OSO 5
22 Jan, 1969
Orbiting Solar
Observatory

OSO 6
9 Aug, 1969
Orbiting Solar
Observatory

SAS 1
12 Dec, 1970
Small Astronomy
Satellite, made x-ray
survey of sky

OSO 7
29 Sept, 1971
Orbiting Solar
Observatory

TD-1A
12 March, 1972
European high
energy
astronomy satellite

OAO 3
21 Aug, 1972
Orbiting
Astronomical
Observatory, for
ultraviolet and x-ray
studies

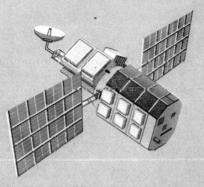

SAS 2
15 Nov, 1972
Small Astronomy
Satellite, made
gamma-ray survey

Ariel V
15 Oct, 1974
UK x-ray satellite

SAS 3
7 May, 1975
Small Astronomy
Satellite, studied
x-ray sources

OSO 8
21 June, 1975
Orbiting Solar
Observatory

HEAO 1
12 Aug, 1977
High Energy
Astronomy
Observatory, made
x-ray survey

IUE
26 Jan, 1978
International
Ultraviolet Explorer,
joint ESA/NASA
satellite

HEAO 2
13 Nov, 1978
High Energy
Astronomy
Observatory
examined
individual x-ray
sources

Ariel VI
2 June, 1979
UK satellite for
cosmic ray and x-ray
studies

HEAO 3
20 Sept, 1979
High Energy
Astronomy
Observatory for
gamma-ray studies

SMM
14 Feb, 1980
Solar Maximum
Mission,
to study the Sun

IRAS
25 Jan, 1983
Infra-red satellite
to provide complete
survey of the sky

Space words

Astronomical unit The average distance from Earth to the Sun, about 150 million km (93 million miles).

Constellation A group of stars which appear to make a shape or pattern in the sky. The stars were joined up to make the outlines of mythical animals or people. There are 88 constellations.

Eclipse This occurs when the Earth passes between the Sun and the Moon and light from the Sun is cut off (a lunar eclipse). It also happens when the Moon passes between the Sun and the Earth, casting a shadow on the Earth (a solar eclipse).

Galaxy A giant group of stars held together by gravity. The largest galaxies contain up to a million, million stars.

Gravity All objects in space attract each other by gravity. It is the invisible pull of the Earth which keeps the Moon in orbit round it, and the pull of the Sun which keeps the Earth and the other planets in their orbits round the Sun.

Light year The distance light travels in one year, 9,460,000 million km (5.9 million, million miles).

Nebula A cloud of gas and dust, sometimes dotted with clusters and stars. Stars may be born in nebulae.

Orbit The curved path taken by a natural or man-made object as it moves round another object.

Planet An object which has no light of its own but shines by reflecting a star's light.

Pulsar Very small, fast-spinning star which sends out a flash of radio waves as it spins round.

Quasar An extremely bright and distant object, much smaller than a galaxy but thousands of times brighter.

Radio telescope A special kind of telescope designed to collect radio waves from space.

Red shift The reddening of the light from a star, indicating it is moving away.

Satellite A natural or artificial object that circles round another. The Moon is a natural satellite of the Earth.

Solar System The system of our Sun. It consists of the nine planets and their moons, the asteroids and comets, all of which orbit the Sun.

Solar wind The high-speed stream of electrically-charged atoms of gas sent out by the Sun.

Star A ball of gas which produces its own heat and light from nuclear reactions at its centre.

Universe Everything which is known or thought to exist in space.

Index